"This is so much to take in," Stephanie said.

Ben crossed the room, his forehead creasing into a small frown. His strides were long and quick as he closed the distance between them. Before she knew it, he'd reached up and clasped her shoulders. Squeezing them gently, he held her.

The warmth of the long, curved hands providing support and understanding was her undoing. She shuddered, and a sob escaped.

Mortified, she tried to pull away, not knowing why the floodgates of Hoover Dam had suddenly opened. Ben wouldn't let her. Pulling her in to his chest, he wrapped his large arms around her. "This has been coming for a long time," he said. "Let it out."

She didn't know what he meant, but his words had the desired effect. Her arms went around him, gripping to keep her from melting to a puddle at his feet, sh

Books by Cheryl Wolverton

Love Inspired

A Matter of Trust #11
A Father's Love #20
This Side of Paradise #38
The Best Christmas Ever #47
A Mother's Love #63
For Love of Zach #76
For Love of Hawk #87
For Love of Mitch #105
Healing Hearts #118
A Husband To Hold #136
In Search of a Hero #166
A Wife for Ben #192

*Hill Creek, Texas

CHERYL WOLVERTON

RITA® Award finalist Cheryl Wolverton has well over a dozen books to her name. Her very popular HILL CREEK, TEXAS, series has been a finalist in many contests. Having grown up in Oklahoma, lived in Kentucky, Texas and now Louisiana, Cheryl and her husband of twenty years and their two children, Jeremiah and Christina, consider themselves Oklahomans who have been transplanted to grow and flourish in the South. Readers are always welcome to contact her via: P.O. Box 207, Slaughter, LA 70777 or e-mail at Cheryl@cherylwolverton.com. You can also visit her Web site at www.cherylwolverton.com.

A Wife for Ben
Cheryl Wolverton

Published by Steeple Hill Books™

STEEPLE HILL BOOKS

Steeple
Hill™

ISBN 0-373-87199-6

A WIFE FOR BEN

Copyright © 2002 by Cheryl Wolverton

This edition published by arrangement with Steeple Hill Books.

Visit us at www.steeplehill.com

Printed in U.S.A.

He will not forget your work and the love
you have shown Him as you helped His people
and continue to help them.

—*Hebrews* 6:10

Writing a book is always a fun process. And the acknowledgments are always something I like to do. I want to thank the librarians—all three of them—from Pride Branch in Pride, Louisiana. They were so helpful in finding the information I needed.

I would like to acknowledge Christina Wolverton. Also Jeremiah Wolverton and my husband, Steve— a wonderful man. Without him, I wouldn't be able to find my computer on some days!

Chapter One

When you think life is going along just fine, life pulls an April fool.
                          —Ben's Laws of Life

I still can't believe it. Here I am, Ben Mayeaux, standing at the altar, about to commit myself to the best person I could have ever met.

Instant family.

I'll have a five-year-old stepdaughter.

Who would have thought?

A staid and sure bachelor at thirty-eight

years old. Not husband material. Not father material. And certainly not hero material.

At least, not until that day that turned my world on its axis like a top out of control...

Let me tell you about it.

Push it, Ben. Almost halfway there.

Sneakered feet pounded the asphalt as Ben Mayeaux worked to make the four miles. Ahead he saw the tree that marked the two miles where he would turn and head back to his house.

It was still dark in the predawn hours in Pride, Louisiana, dark and already humid. A thick early-morning fog was starting to build and cover the road where he ran, filling the wooded pine forests around him, making his feet echo hollowly as he pounded onward.

Come on, Ben. You can do it, just like when you were twenty. So, what if you're thirty-eight, nearly thirty-nine. You're at your best right now, at your prime. You have everything in life you want.

In and out, in and out, his breathing continued, if a bit labored.

He might feel like he was still twenty, but

his body was telling him he should have called it quits at the mile marker.

He reached the turnaround point and headed down the road, inhaling the scent of crisp budding pines and exhaling in cadence with his running.

Pace yourself, Ben. You can do it.

Inhale…pound, pound, pound…exhale…pound, pound, pound.

Inhale…pound, pound… What was that smell? He continued another mile inhaling and exhaling, inhaling and exhaling, as the smell got stronger.

Distracted by the scent of wood burning so early on a spring morning, Ben slowed, glancing about. Stumbling to a halt, he bent, dropping his hands to his knees and inhaling as he tried to catch his breath. The odd smell was a good excuse to stop, and he didn't have to admit he wasn't as young as he used to be.

Ah, age. The wonderful joys of it. He was satisfied with all he had, where he was in life and everything else. But his body told him he was getting older.

Lifting his head, he again inhaled.

Yeah. Definitely wood smoke.

He wondered who would be outside burning trash or dead trees this early in the morning. The haze of dawn was just rearing its head. Walking forward to cool down until he caught his breath, he glanced around, speculating just who else might be up this early.

The road was deserted except for the shift workers who left around five to make it into Baton Rouge for shift change. Soon he'd be seeing buses as the local schools got ready to pick up kids for class. Then the everyday crowd of cars heading into Baton Rouge, the only place that really had a job market around, would finally start making its way toward town.

Pride, with a population of a few thousand, and neighboring Zachary, with less than ten thousand, certainly couldn't support themselves.

So most folks traveled into Baton Rouge for work.

Taking a deep inhalation of the muggy morning he searched again, wondering just who might be up. It was possible a straight day, eight-to-five worker had some chores that needed doing and was performing them before he left for work.

But Ben didn't have that many neighbors. Along this road there were maybe six houses in a six-mile area.

A haze caught his attention. That way, he realized, spotting where the haze drifted from. He instinctively started off the road toward the nearest neighbor he had. A woman lived there, if he remembered correctly. He'd seen her out occasionally in the evening when he ran. She was usually taking out trash or heading into the house. Sometimes he'd spotted her trying to clear out the front garden.

A cold chill worked its way up his sweat-covered body as he walked partway up the two-hundred-yard driveway. It wasn't like him to interfere with neighbors. He was a bachelor and a loner and liked it that way. But he couldn't picture this woman out at dawn burning excess wood as she cleared away her yard. And if that wasn't enough to cause his unease to grow, the fact that few people had fireplaces and those that did didn't use them in springtime—unless they were crazy—really caused his spine to tingle with foreboding.

He'd just take a quick peek to see what she was doing and make sure she was okay and...

And call for help, he realized as he saw smoke billowing from the side of the house.

The back part of the house was in flames.

His heart leaped to his throat as he realized he was witnessing a house fire. He rushed to the front door and pounded on it. The sound of crackling flames could be heard echoing in the early-morning stillness.

Ben couldn't perceive any movement inside the house. He hit the doorbell, then quickly pounded again. ''Fire! Get up!'' he called.

Impatiently he stood on his toes to peek in the door window.

He should call the fire department, but it was over a mile to his house. And he knew the woman had to be in there, most likely asleep. Her car was in the driveway.

Glancing around, he saw a flowerpot on her front porch.

He grabbed it and slammed it through the spacious front bay window. ''Anyone home? Fire!'' he called, all the while clearing the glass from around the frame with the red clay pot.

As soon as he had a spot cleared, he shoved back the curtains and climbed in. The semidark living room was scattered with old furniture including a couch that he stumbled over. Across from him were the kitchen and a window that showed the backyard. No one was in sight.

The smell of smoke hung in the warm air. A clock ticked loudly. Ben covered his mouth and nose with his hand and rushed toward the hallway, certain the woman would be down that way, more certain than ever that she had to be in trouble, otherwise she would have answered by now.

''Fire! Get out!'' he shouted, choking on his words as the acrid smell hit him. He saw a phone on a small table next to the entrance to the hall, snatched it up and dialed 911 before dropping it and continuing. He knew someone would respond, since the number had been dialed. That was enough.

Down the hall the smoke was thicker. Something out back was on fire, and this was the side of the house affected, he thought dimly. Suddenly the fire alarm in the front room started blaring.

If anyone was asleep, that would wake him or her up, he thought, glancing through the smoke, wanting to believe no one was there, that surely he was overreacting. His eyes burned and watered from the thickening smoke. Still, he was able to see enough to spot a closed door.

He started toward the closed door a few feet away. He had only taken two steps when his foot snagged something on the floor.

With a grunt he went down hard on the carpet, skinning both knees. Turning, feeling for what he'd tripped over, his hands met with flesh.

It was a woman. The woman, he realized. The one he was looking for. Enshrouded in pink pajamas, the woman lay still, one arm outstretched, her blond hair covering her face, keeping him from seeing it.

The smoke intensified and choked him. Galvanized, he worked to get the woman in his arms. Coughing, his eyes watering and burning, he grabbed her limp arm and swung her over his shoulder.

A gasp and raspy cough broke from his bundle. He felt relief to know she was still alive.

He headed toward the front door. The heat had already increased drastically.

"No." She coughed. He could hardly hear the feminine voice over the blaring sound of the alarm as he rushed through the living room.

"Fire, ma'am," Ben said.

The woman started fighting him.

"Be still, I don't want to drop you." He shifted her weight and anchored her firmly, visions of dropping her and not making it out of the house flashing in his mind.

He reached the door and fumbled with the lock, then jerked it open and rushed out. Air, clean and plentiful, met them. He got away from the house and deposited his bundle on the ground, working to breathe and clear his lungs.

"No! No…" The woman gagged, her raspy voice barely audible between the hoarseness and coughing. Out of the soot-covered face, two deep blue eyes pleaded with him, terrified, desperate. Her hands gripped his arm as she sucked in air, trying to calm her coughing.

"You've inhaled smoke. You need to lie still."

"You—under—and. Baby…"

Ben's heart dropped at her words. His breath stuck in his throat.

"Baby? Someone else is in the house?"

Frantically she nodded, her black-streaked hair falling into her face. "Five. I have—her." She broke into another round of coughing.

Ben's stomach clenched with queasiness. Whirling, he stared at the house. Flames engulfed the back part. The roof was smoldering and would go at any time. In the distance he heard the sound of sirens, but with all the smoke and fire, they wouldn't make it in time.

He didn't think. He simply acted. Taking a deep breath, he barreled into the house. Thick billowing smoke met him, and he prayed he'd find the child before he choked on the noxious odors.

Think. Think!

The woman, lying in the floor near a door. Yes. That was it. She had to be going after her daughter. Rushing that way, Ben met scorching heat. Putting his hand to the door he found it warm, not hot, and hoped it was safe to open without causing damage.

With a quick jerk, he opened and closed it behind him. Smoke, not as thick, had started filling this room. Wiping an arm across his sweat-covered face, he called, "Anyone here? Come out. We have to get you out of here."

He broke into a round of coughing, feeling as if his lungs were on fire. He could hardly make out the bed across the room—only enough to see the covers were disturbed, as if someone had been in it.

He jerked the closet door open, found no one. A quick move around the room. He was getting frantic. He couldn't breathe. The heat was intense against the door. He was out of time.

As a last shot he went to the bed and suddenly realized he hadn't looked under it. Sure enough, a small child was bundled under there, crying. He heard her as soon as he went down on one knee. Brown curly hair surrounded the child's fearful face. Big brown eyes, filled with fright, locked on to him. In her arms she held a white teddy bear. Her breathing was uneven and labored as she stared at him, frozen under her bed.

"Come here, honey," Ben said, and without waiting for a reply grabbed her. She dropped the bear, her arms clutching at his neck, to his ever-lasting relief. "It's gonna be okay, sweet-heart. We'll get you outta here."

The little girl whimpered in his ear, clutching his neck and burying her head against his shoulder.

A sense of purpose took over him. He'd get this little girl out.

The door was too hot, out of the question to go back that way, so he chose the window. Covering her with the blanket from the bed, he went to the window. Using his hands, he managed to get the glass out, then kicked out the screen. The mother was on the other side of the window, unsteady but working to help. Her deep blue eyes were determined and steady. She wanted her child out of the burning house and in her arms.

He'd never seen that look in a woman's eyes before. It was a mother's willingness to do anything to protect her child.

He gladly handed the coughing child to her mother before slipping through the small square exit and landing unsteadily in the flower garden, going to one knee. He forced himself to his feet, slipped an arm around the tiny frame of the mother and pushed her farther from the house. ''Others?'' He rasped the word out, trying to breathe in the warm muggy morning air but feeling like he was breathing in razors over raw skin.

''No. None. Oh…'' Gasp, cough. ''Thank you.'' Hugging her child closely to her chest, she dropped to her knees.

Between her sobs and her coughs, Ben couldn't make out much of what the pink-enshrouded woman said. Falling to his knees, he knelt and worked on breathing.

The crunching of gravel as a fire truck pulled in mixed with the sound of the corner of the roof collapsing on the house.

In what seemed like seconds a fireman was beside them administering first aid, giving them oxygen and easing their painful attempts to breathe.

Ben watched the ambulance arrive. Technicians checked out each of them. He noted that the woman, her long blond hair smudged with soot, clung to her daughter. The little child, who had dark hair and big brown eyes, looked like the mother except in coloring. She looked more scared than ill from the smoke.

The technicians took no chances and gave

the child oxygen. Then it was his turn. The two ambulance technicians worked on them as the firemen shouted back and forth, spraying water on the fire to get it under control.

Finally, with the woman on a stretcher and the child and Ben strapped into seats across from her, the ambulance headed for the hospital in Zachary.

Over and over he heard the woman saying, "Thank you. Thank you. Thank you." And the entire time, as he watched the woman try to comfort the child and be brave while coping with the fact she'd just lost most of her house and nearly her life, he thought, Where's your husband?

Chapter Two

> *Women are a species all to themselves,*
> *with the ability to cause you to make*
> *crazy decisions.*
>
> —Ben's Laws of Life

Okay, okay, I admit I was ashamed not to know my neighbors. But when you see a good-looking woman with a kid you expect to find a husband attached.

At least I did. Of course, I was going to find out many of my bachelor ideas were inaccurate, to say the least. But first, I had to learn just how out of touch with the real world I was.

And boy did I get a dose of reality right after we arrived at the hospital.

"You don't know her name?"

Ben shrugged. "No." He could feel the dull flush creep up his cheeks as the nurse inspected him like he was some odd microbe under a microscope. Turning to the bed next to him, he asked, "Can you tell me your name?"

He wondered why the nurse had asked him instead of the woman, anyway.

Through the oxygen mask she wore the woman muttered, "Nie...ebber."

Glancing at the nurse, he said, "Annie Webber." He remembered the name Webber on the mailbox.

The nurse studied him. "This *is* your wife, sir?"

Shaking his head, he admitted, "No. We're not married."

The woman next to him grabbed his hand.

"I see," the nurse said, looking pointedly at their hands.

"St...nie," the woman said, jerking on his hand.

The little girl, who shared a bed with her

mother, got down from the cot and moved next to Ben. She grasped his jogging sock.

Ben glanced from the woman's hand, which was soot-covered, to the small child, who was suddenly hanging on him, and imagined just what the nurse thought she saw. "No, you don't understand. I don't know—" He started coughing.

The nurse tsked and adjusted the mask on his face then lifted the little girl to sit next to him.

He stared at the child, trying to figure out just why the nurse would put her there.

The little girl smiled beatifically then pulled at her mask, adjusting it, before leaning against him.

"St—nn—nie." The woman stuttered again, drawing his attention from the alienlike being who'd just claimed one of his arms as her own.

This was unreal, he thought, looking from the woman to the child to the smirking nurse.

"I was jogging and came upon the—" His voice broke as he fell into a fresh spasm of coughs.

The nurse adjusted his mask again—and then slipped the clipboard under her arm. "Just relax. Breathe in and let the oxygen do its work. Give me a license and I'll have the desk clerk finish this, Mr....?''

''I don't have a license,'' he said between gasps. ''I told you. I was jog—''

''Ah, here is the doctor now.'' The nurse didn't act as if she cared that he hadn't gotten to give her a lick of information. Instead, she was all business as she nodded toward the man who'd entered the room.

A young man full of energy strode into the curtained area where the three of them sat—or rather two sat and one lay, he thought, glancing at Annie.

''We're going to get some X rays and do some blood gases and then, most likely, you can go home.'' He went from Annie, checking her eyes and fingernails, to Ben and then the child. He paused long enough to listen to their hearts and lungs. Ben gratefully used that time to catch his breath and relax so his throat would stop clenching in pain against his attempts to talk.

''No burns,'' the doctor said, nodding approvingly. ''That's good. From what the techs say, you guys were really lucky getting out of the house when you did.'' He didn't ask questions or stop to get to know the three of them. Instead, he offered a smile and added, ''Don't you worry now, everything will be fine.'' With a quick nod he replied, ''Gotta run. Busy morning. By the way, you have a cute daughter,'' he added to Ben as he strode out.

''She's not—''

The nurse followed the doctor.

Ben raised his hand to stop her and then gave up. He leaned back on the bed and realized the child still clung to him.

Glancing at her, uneasy at such a close proximity to something so small, he wondered what he was supposed to do with her. His niece and nephew never clung like this.

''Katie?'' The woman reached toward the child, forcing herself into a sitting position.

The little girl wiggled and moved into her mother's arms. The mother bowed her head over the girl and shuddered. Finally, she looked up. Through the mask she said, once again, ''Thank you.''

He shrugged. ''I'm glad you made it out okay.'' He found breathing became easier as he relaxed.

"I have no idea what happened," the woman said. "I woke up. Having…bad dream and smelled…smoke. I thought Katie…" She shuddered and squeezed her daughter. Bowing her head, she gasped as if fighting tears. "I have no idea what we're going to do. My house burned down. We don't have family here."

"No husband?" Ben asked then flushed, realizing that wasn't something he should ask. But surely she had a husband. She had a kid.

"No. No husband."

The woman was alone.

"No one to stay with?" he asked. Aw, man, for some reason this just didn't sound right. A woman wasn't supposed to live isolated from all of her family. Everyone had family. Even he had a sister who lived over in Slaughter, just north of Zachary.

"No. I mean…" He could see she was trying to think of someone. "I guess I could find someone…maybe. I don't know.…"

It was the tears that did it.

He knew when he saw those tears no matter what happened at the hospital, he was going to make sure this woman was okay once she left.

First one, then another tear slipped over her cheeks, past the mask to run down her neck, leaving clean streaks through her darkened face.

He couldn't handle tears. He'd never been able to handle tears. ''You can stay at my house until we can get to your home tomorrow and make sure you can move back in,'' he said, though he didn't think she'd be able to move in that quickly. They'd have to check the damage. ''By the way,'' he added belatedly, ''I'm your neighbor, Ben.''

The woman glanced up, the surprise in her face mirroring what he felt.

What was he doing? He was a bachelor. He didn't have time for people—especially people of the female sort or the small sort. He hadn't just invited a woman and kid to share his house, had he? No way would he do something so stupid.

It was impossible.

But sitting there, staring at the woman and child, at the look of utter helplessness on her face as she continued to struggle to breathe, Ben realized his major weakness was a woman in peril. His sister swore he couldn't say no to a woman. And here was this young mother needing help. How could he turn them away?

He couldn't.

It was that simple.

With an inward sigh he admitted he'd done it. He'd invited them to stay with him. And he wasn't going to take no for an answer.

What was he getting himself into?

Chapter Three

*Bachelorhood is simply a way of saying
I don't know anything about women.*
                                        —Ben's Laws of Life

There had been a ton of paperwork to sign,
and even though the doctor had seen them they
still had tests that needed doing. While the
nurses had been busy poking and prodding,
Stephanie had asked about calling a taxi, but
Ben had insisted on calling his friend.

She was glad for the ride. She couldn't afford a taxi, and even if she could pay for a
cab, where would she go? She had been honest

when she'd said she couldn't think of anyone to stay with. She was still probing her mind for someone who might have room to put her up for a day or two. She wasn't sure what she could do. She'd had a house and now she didn't. At least, she didn't think she did. It had been burning when they'd left.

When they'd finally straightened everything out with the paperwork and it was time for a signature, Ben's friend had shown up.

"I'm certain that it'll be fine if you stay with me until we get something done with your house," Ben said, and Stephanie felt herself redden in the early-morning light. "The doctor said it'd be a good idea for all of us to rest today, and you certainly aren't going to do that back at your house. I'll have John go by and board up what he can and tomorrow you can look at it."

Confused, Stephanie asked, "Board up?"

He nodded. "Cover whatever there is left to cover. The entire house didn't burn down. There'll be things you can salvage. We'll need to call the insurance company, of course, but everything else can wait until tomorrow. You had a close call this morning."

Ben Mayeaux. It suddenly clicked who this man was.

"I've heard a lot about you. I mean, you aren't exactly a stranger, Mr. Mayeaux."

Stephanie knew that sounded like an odd thing to say to a man she'd really never met. But as they drove back from Lane Hospital, she couldn't help but chat to cover her nervousness. And she was nervous. Why had she accepted his invitation? Though she said she knew something about him, she only knew the basic facts. He was her neighbor, lived alone but was more involved in the community than she was. Everyone around town said he was a very nice person and really cared about people—even if he was a bit of a loner.

"Oh?" he asked, though the wary look that crossed his face told his true feelings.

"I know you're at all of the town meetings and are on the board to build a better school even though you don't have children. You're quiet and keep to yourself and build stuff."

"I build houses, Annie."

"Stephanie," she corrected.

"Yeah," he murmured. His voice still sounded hoarse from the smoke.

''Thank you again,'' she whispered. She reached up and rubbed her throat, thinking it felt raw as she talked.

''You've said that before,'' he countered lightly.

She squeezed her daughter closer to her side. She didn't think she would ever stop saying thank-you. The fear that had consumed her as she'd realized the house was on fire and her daughter was down the hall—her heart pounded just remembering the terror.

''I won't get tired of saying it. You saved my daughter's life.'' She felt tears come again as she said those words.

The man driving the car rolled his eyes. Ben Mayeaux stiffened with unease.

Bachelors, she could tell. Not used to women, but she couldn't help it. Her child had almost died. This man had saved them. ''You're my daughter's hero. I can't thank you enough for what you did.''

''Yeah. Well...'' Ben shifted uncomfortably.

Stephanie cleared her throat. ''I know we're supposed to rest, but is there any way...I mean...'' She shrugged, holding her daughter as close as the seat belts would allow. "I really need to stop and see my house today. Just to assure myself. I know it sounds crazy but..."

"No, it doesn't." Ben turned to the driver. "John, let's stop by there first. But it'll only be for a few minutes," he added without looking at her.

Stephanie felt duly reprimanded for disobeying doctor's orders. But she just had to see her house. The fire hadn't been out when they'd left. She couldn't explain why it was so important, but she just had to see, to make sure something was there. The fire seemed almost like a dream.

John turned onto the Pride-Port Hudson road before taking another turn onto a road that led to the house.

The first thing she noticed was that there were still small clouds of smoke hanging over the house, coming up in thin spirals from some blackened wood to the side of where her daughter's room used to be.

The second thing she noticed was that part of her roof was missing.

John pulled into the driveway, the gravel

crunching underneath the tires as he rolled to a stop.

"Mama," Katie whimpered and pointed.

"It's okay, honey," Stephanie said, though it wasn't.

She released her seat belt and pushed open the car door.

The smell of burned wood permeated the air, making her daughter wrinkle her nose.

As Stephanie started toward the house, Ben warned, "Don't go inside. We don't know what's secure."

Katie clung to her mother's hand. Stephanie trembled as they walked to the side of the house past the many azaleas and hydrangeas, past the hawthorns and bridal-wreath bushes to where their bedrooms were located. The garden that had contained her flowering perennials had been crushed and was covered with soot. The annuals were gone, trampled and destroyed in the attempts to get her daughter and put out the fire. The walls to the bedrooms had been severely damaged, especially Katie's room.

Her stomach turned, and she felt queasy as

she saw how much damage Katie's room had sustained.

Her daughter wouldn't have lived had Ben waited for the firemen to get her out.

"Thank you, God," she whispered, shuddering.

Katie tugged on her hand, slipped free and ran toward the blackened wood.

"Katie! Watch out. It's dangerous there."

"My bear, Mama," she said, and squatted in the mess that had once been the outside wall to her room.

Stephanie hurried after her and got to her just as she stood.

Sure enough, black-coated but amazingly not too wet or burned, was the white teddy Katie liked to sleep with.

The little girl pounded the bear on the ground. "She's dirty."

"She sure is," Ben said, walking up. "We can wash her out at my house," he offered.

Stephanie wasn't sure how well the bear would fare being washed, but she didn't argue. Instead she said, "Mr. Ben is right. We can clean it all up."

If only she could say the same thing about

the house, she thought as her daughter ran toward the car to show John what she'd found.

Katie didn't know what a stranger was.

Stephanie surveyed the rest of the house from where she stood.

Ben walked next to her. "It's not as bad as it looks."

"It looks pretty bad," she said and laughed. It was not a laugh of joy but of welling despair. It was a laugh with a touch of sarcasm, a laugh that escaped to cover the tears that would come otherwise.

She had the oddest feeling Ben knew that as he slipped an arm around her and gave her shoulders a hug.

"We'll come back tomorrow and go through everything. Just from this side it looks like the fire started toward the back and spread. I guess breaking your daughter's window gave the fire enough oxygen to really destroy her room, but I'd be willing to bet the rest of the house is intact, if not a little water- and smoke-damaged."

"I don't know," she murmured. "Standing here..."

"You need to rest."

Glancing at the man beside her, she realized he was right. She was numb.

He was very perceptive.

Studying him, she realized he wasn't feeling as well as he sounded, either. "Does your throat hurt as much as mine does?"

A crooked grin tilted one corner of his mouth. "I don't know. How much does your throat hurt?"

"Feels like a rusty railroad track, and the train derailed somewhere along the line," she admitted.

He chuckled. "Come on. Let's go to the house. You can take one of those pills the doctor gave you—after you shower."

"Clothes!" she said, suddenly realizing all she had were the pajamas she was dressed in.

Ben glanced down, realizing what she was wearing.

"Ah, um..." He stepped away from her, looking acutely uncomfortable. "You can borrow one of my shirts. You really shouldn't go in there until we're certain how stable the structure is. And your daughter, well, can she wear a T-shirt maybe?"

He acted like he was embarrassed or unsure

of the offer. To her it sounded like a lifeline. "Thank you—again," she said.

He nodded.

"Let's go," he said firmly but gently.

She nodded and headed to the car. "Thank you again," she whispered as she started to climb in the car.

Ben smiled and said as he shut her door, "We're going to have to talk about this thank-you thing."

She thought they could talk, but after seeing what her daughter's former bedroom looked like, she'd never get tired of saying it.

No matter what he said.

Chapter Four

Family are the people who know everything about you and are willing to comment on everything even if it's not their business.

—Ben's Laws of Life

"Do you need to call your boss? Maybe some friends to let them know you're okay?"

Ben stood in the living room watching the way the little girl, Katie, clung to her mom as her mom hung up the phone from the insurance company and then dialed Katie's school. She had said those were the two calls she had to make. He thought it was strange that she didn't call friends or a boss. They looked so odd standing there in his kitchen, covered with soot, dirtying his phone. The child clung to the mother and the grimy teddy bear clutched to her chest with equal desperation.

He wondered what the two saw in his house. Trying to see it through their eyes, he noted the stark wood furniture with the brown cushions. A large tan rug covered part of the polished wooden floor in the lower section of the living room where he stood.

Various pads and pencils were tossed on the coffee table and end tables. The shelf over the fireplace was empty except for a few gifts his sister had gotten him—mugs, a picture of her, her husband and two kids.

There were no knickknacks or crocheted table covers like his grandmother had had sprinkled all over her house. He had some in a box somewhere that he'd gotten when Grandma Betsy had died, but he'd never bothered to unpack them.

He hadn't understood their use—until now.

The house looked sort of bare without such things.

"No. I mean, there's the church, but then there's not a lot they can do—except maybe clothes and food—after I figure out what I'll need. As for friends, well..." She shrugged. "And, well, I'm my own boss, actually. I do ad campaigns for businesses. Art and things like that. Graphics. I also do Web sites." She shrugged and replaced the phone in the cradle, which rested on the wall near the kitchen.

He was glad he tended to keep a clean—if empty—house. The kitchen had a couple of dirty dishes in the sink, but that was it. The dining room table in front of the patio doors was spotless except for a few more pads of paper.

Suddenly, he smiled triumphantly. There were place mats there—the ones his sister had bought him last Christmas.

Realizing the woman was staring at him, he said, "That's interesting. You know, I was thinking of hiring someone to create a Web page for me and work up an ad. My business has been picking up this last year, and I wanted to focus on expanding it through the media."

It was the truth.

It was also an invitation for her to talk. He couldn't remember the last time he'd felt this awkward around a woman. Seeing her there in her pink frilly pajamas... Oh man, he thought, and almost slapped his head as he realized he'd made her and her daughter continue to stand there, soot-covered, in their pajamas.

"It's important you have an idea what you want before you get started. Perhaps I could give you some advice," she offered.

He walked up to the second level of the house, went to the hall and started down it. "I'd like that."

"Can you perhaps give me an idea how much the repairs might be to the house? I have insurance but I know there's going to be some out-of-pocket expense. You do those things, so maybe you have an idea?"

He listened to her voice as he dug through his closet and found two shirts. He stopped at the linen closet and dug out towels. She sounded just as nervous as he did, he realized.

He returned to the living room and set his plunder on the table. "Tell you what," he said, thinking to relax the woman a bit. He had a very bad feeling she was strapped for money. Maybe it was because the pajamas she wore were faded and frayed around the wrists and ankles. Or maybe it was the fact that the little kid's gown was about three inches too short, both on the legs and arms. "Would you consider doing up a campaign for me if I waived the repair job costs?"

He'd said something wrong, he realized immediately from the way she stiffened. Lifting his hands in a conciliatory gesture, he offered, "We'll draw up a contract. It'll be strictly business. But as I was saying earlier, I sure could use some advice on that expansion John and I are planning."

She hesitated then relaxed. "Let's discuss that."

Relieved she hadn't taken him to task for the crazy offer, he nodded. "Sounds good."

Rubbing at his throat, he went into the kitchen. "I hope you'll make yourself at home. Just help yourself if you want drinks or food. I'll warn you, I'm not the best host in the world. I'm a workaholic," he ruefully admitted. "I plan to call my company, take a shower and then rest for a while. I'd suggest you two do the same.''

He opened the medication the doctor gave him for pain and downed two pills. He got a glass out of the cabinet next to the sink, slid it into the refrigerator door and filled it up, quickly swallowing the cold water.

At the giggle from the little kid, he turned his head, curious. ''You got water out of there,'' she informed him.

He blinked. ''Yeah.''

''She's never seen one of those before,'' Stephanie said.

''Oh.'' Shifting, he shrugged. Deciding to try to win the child's friendship, he went to the cupboard and pulled out another glass. ''You want to try?''

Her eyes lit up as if he'd offered her candy. She scampered across the room and grabbed the glass.

''Push it up against this, like so,'' he said, and helped her.

''I can do it,'' she informed him immediately and then pushed like he'd showed her and watched the water fill the glass—and overflow.

"Oh, dear," Stephanie said, coming forward.

"No problem," Ben said. "Why don't you two go take a quick shower and I'll wipe up the spill?"

Stephanie nodded. "Come on, Katie," she said and slipping her hands to her daughter's shoulders hurried her off.

Ben shook his head, found a cloth and wiped up the water running down the refrigerator.

Well, that had been an interesting almost conversation, he thought sardonically.

He hoped things eased between them or this was going to be a long few days.

He tossed the cloth into the sink, made a quick call to his office then headed for his room and the shower. It'd been a long morning, and surprisingly all he wanted to do was take a nice long cool shower and then get some shut-eye.

Unfortunately, as he was climbing out of the tub his phone kept him from doing just that. He grabbed a pair of pajama bottoms, slipped into them then snagged the phone.

"Hello?" Cradling the phone between his

shoulder and ear, he tied the drawstring and listened.

"Hi, Ben, it's me, Sunni. Are you okay?"

Ben resisted the urge to sigh. He reached for a comb and quickly ran it through his hair before dropping to the bed next to him. "I'm fine. Why do you ask?" He lay the comb on the bedside table.

Of course, he knew why she was asking about him. He should have known she'd have heard by now, especially the way word traveled in small towns, but he just hadn't had time to think. No excuse—well, maybe two, which were in the other room sleeping right now.

"I called your office to ask about dinner Sunday, and John said you'd nearly been killed in a fire. Why didn't you call me? I nearly fainted dead away over what John said!"

His sister tended to exaggerate a bit. The utter shock and excitement in her voice told him she was hyped up over this. He hadn't meant to upset her so. Working to calm her down, he reassured her. "It's okay, Sunni. My neighbor's house caught fire. She, her daughter and I are fine."

He didn't want to say he'd gone inside if she didn't know.

"You went in after them."

Oh, well. So much for her not knowing that. He was really in for it now. She took a breath, not waiting for him to answer, and continued with her tirade.

"Are you crazy? Ben, that's what firemen are trained to do, not citizens. I mean…" She paused.

He heard her take a deep breath. "You're my only brother. I could have lost you."

At the waver in her voice, he realized she was going to cry. Worried at that sound, the one sound that could cripple him, that sound that would bring any man to his knees, he knew he had to divert her, and quick. "Annie and her daughter are staying here. Katie is five, about Ronnie's size," he said.

"*Veronica* is six."

"I know, but when I saw Katie I thought of Ronnie."

"You and that infernal nickname," Sunni muttered, no longer sounding in tears but put out with him. Relieved, he relaxed a bit.

"I wondered if you—"

"Wait a minute."

He paused. "What?"

"You have a woman and child staying with you?"

She'd gone from crying to incredulous in under thirty seconds. That was his Sunni. "Yeah. They couldn't very well stay in their house until they knew how bad the damage was. The doctor wanted to give them some medicine to help them rest and they would have had to stay in the hospital otherwise."

"Doesn't she have friends?"

Ben paused, stumped. "To be honest, I don't know. She was in shock over her house. I was there. I offered."

"She cried, didn't she?"

Ben scowled at the phone. "I'm her neighbor," he informed his nosy sister. "It was the right thing to do."

"Well, that's nice, Ben. I'm sure it is. But if they're staying there... I mean, what are they doing about toiletries and clothes and—"

"Do you have any old clothes that Katie could borrow until tomorrow when we can go over to her house? I know it's asking a lot, but—"

"No, it's not. I'll go through Veronica's stuff and come right—"

"Over this evening." He cut in, trying to slow his sister down. He'd diverted her into her helping mode. He usually shunned that mode of Sunni's, but considering the alternative, he felt this was a great distraction.

"I'll bring supper. David is offshore, working, and won't be back for a few more days so I'd love to bring food over to eat. I hope you don't mind. I mean, I know you're not used to cooking for more than yourself."

Ben realized his sister was right. A yawn caught him off guard. "Yeah. That sounds good, sis. Listen, I took some medication the doctor gave me and it's kicking in. Can we discuss this around six o'clock tonight?"

"I'll be there. And Ben?"

"Yeah?" he asked, shoving the covers back and reseating himself.

"I'm glad you're okay."

"Me, too, sis."

"I love you."

"You too."

"Bye."

"Bye."

He cradled the phone in its place and slipped under the covers. Talking with his sister was like a roller coaster ride of emotions. She was a very energetic person who cared deeply about him.

Raised by their elderly grandmother, he and Sunni shared a special relationship.

Being dropped off that day together, all alone, with just a suitcase of clothes had forced them to share a tighter bond than most siblings.

He should have called her first thing after he got home.

He couldn't believe he'd forgotten to do so.

Shaking his head, he allowed himself to relax, promising he'd make it up to her later tonight—when she came over for supper.

Chapter Five

One female in a bachelor's household is disconcerting, two or more you just might as well give up and accept the inevitability of disaster.

—Ben's Laws of Life

A giggle woke her.

Thinking it was her daughter, Stephanie rolled over and opened her eyes.

A boy, perhaps four or five, stood beside her bed, a big grin on his face, two crooked teeth sticking out as he smiled.

Dark brown eyes sparkled with mischief.

"Well, hello," she said, shifting to sit up.

"That's Justin. I'm Veronica."

Stephanie glanced at the door where an older version of the child in front of her stood. The older child had perfectly straight teeth and long brown curly hair. "It's nice to meet you. I'm Stephanie."

"Uncle Ben said you were Annie. He asked me to bring you this dress that Mom brought over."

In her hands she held a dark blue housedress—strings tied at the throat, short sleeves with a stretchy waist. It didn't look like something she'd wear, but she was so very grateful for any feminine clothing she knew she would put it on and be happy with it.

"Thank you." Stephanie accepted the dress from the girl.

"Mama brought dinner. Katie is already in there."

"My daughter?"

Veronica grinned. "She's helping Mama set the table. I got out of it because she wanted to do it. Uncle Ben said to let you sleep some until dinner."

''I see. Well, then, why don't you run on and tell him I'm up and I'll be right there, okay?''

''Okay. Come on, Justin.''

She walked over and grabbed her brother's hand.

''I wanna stay.''

''You can't. She has to put her dress on,'' the older sister ordered.

Justin didn't argue but followed his sister out.

Stephanie quickly took off the shirt Ben had given her and slipped the dress on, trying to regain her equilibrium. She wasn't used to waking up in a stranger's house with unfamiliar children staring at her. To find out her daughter was with strangers was even more disconcerting.

She quickly brushed her hair and left the room, still barefoot but at least covered and semipresentable.

As she entered the living room she caught sight of Ben handing the silverware to his sister, who handed it to Katie. Stephanie paused and watched as her daughter carefully began laying out the forks and then knives and spoons. Everything else was on the table.

And it smelled delicious.

"Oh, you must be Annie," a tall, willowy woman said from the kitchen. She came forward, reached out and hugged Stephanie.

"Actually, it's Stephanie," Stephanie corrected, accepting the hug.

"Stephanie?" She glanced at her brother in query then at Stephanie. "You poor thing. I heard what happened." She reached for Stephanie and took her hand and squeezed it, then continued to hold it. "I'm Sunni, Ben's older sister. I live over in Slaughter. When I understood what straits you were in I had to help. Hope you like smothered chicken and okra." After releasing Stephanie's hand, she motioned toward the table.

Stephanie nodded, her stomach grumbling in welcome of a meal. "It smells wonderful. I can't believe I slept the day away." *Straits?* She wondered just what Sunni meant by that statement and what Ben had told her.

She was also embarrassed that it was already dinnertime and she hadn't awakened once during the day. Right now, however, what she really wanted was something to drink. Her throat still hurt, a painful reminder of the catastrophe that morning. But not just her throat hurt, she realized suddenly. For some reason so did the muscles in her arms and legs and back. Actually, she felt as if she'd run a marathon.

"Why don't we go ahead and sit down and eat then," Sunni said, interrupting Stephanie's musings.

Ben dried his hands on a towel and crossed toward the dining room table. "I hear you met Sunni's children." He patted Sunni's daughter on the shoulder as he passed her and rubbed Justin's head. "Her husband, David, is offshore right now." He stopped behind a chair, pulled it out and glanced at her. "I don't know about you, but I'm ready to eat."

Stephanie quickly crossed to the chair and allowed herself to be seated, surprised at the gesture but feeling oddly flustered.

Ben positioned himself next to his sister and then watched as the kids quietly pulled their napkins out and slipped them into their laps.

Well behaved, she'd give the kids that.

They immediately started dishing out food,

however, which caused a problem with her daughter. Katie wasted no time in advising them how they had violated her routine. "Wait!"

Ben, who had just reached for the bread, paused, his eyes wide in surprise.

Stephanie blushed, not sure what to say. She knew exactly what the problem was.

"What is it, Katie?" Sunni asked before Stephanie had a chance to say a word.

"We can do it silently," Stephanie offered.

Ben looked from one to the other. "Do what?"

"You didn't pray," Katie said, accusation in her voice. "You can't eat until you do."

It was obvious none of the others at the table had ever said grace before a meal. Sunni, however, smiled. "What a nice idea. Okay. Let's pray. How do we do this now?"

Shocked, Stephanie thought surely Sunni was kidding. But the others didn't look like she was kidding. Instead, they all stared at Katie.

"You have to bow your head like this." Katie demonstrated by lowering her head until her chin touched her chest. She folded her hands and crooked her head, one eye opened and staring at them as she continued. "Then you close your eyes so no one can see you. Then you just talk."

When she was certain they understood she scrunched her eyes shut. "Thank you, God, for this food. And that we aren't hurt. And for Mommie and Mr. Ben and he saved our lives. Amen."

Stephanie hadn't been able to bow her head, she had been so stunned. She noted that Sunni had imitated Katie, as had her children. Ben belatedly tried to bow his head, but it was too late. With a sheepish glance at his sister he shifted the napkin in his lap.

"Amen," Sunni echoed. "That's very good manners, Katie. Do you think we can eat now?"

The sweet smile on Sunni's face caused a reciprocal one to form on Katie's. "Now we can."

Sunni clapped. "Okay, everyone."

Stephanie felt like apologizing but at the same time she was proud of her daughter. She hadn't known what to do when they'd started to eat. Her daughter, however, hadn't hesitated. And on top of that, Sunni had praised her.

Glancing up, she found Ben staring at her. He offered her a crooked smile. Relaxing, she decided to go on from there. She took a long sip of water, easing her dry throat, before accepting the chicken that was passed to her. She dished herself up something to eat.

"Did you teach Katie to do that, Stephanie?" Sunni asked as she passed the bread from her brother to Stephanie, pausing to put a piece on Justin's plate.

"I suppose. It's just something we've always done. Even at our church suppers we pray before our meals."

"Oh. You go to church," Sunni said, and started to cut up her son's food.

"Yes. Down the road in Zachary, actually."

"We're not into church or religion," Sunni confessed. "I guess I've never thought about it."

She couldn't believe Sunni had never been to church. "Never?"

"Well, we've been to a couple of funerals. But my husband and I were married by a justice of the peace. I've never been to Sunday service.''

Ben interrupted. ''Our grandmother didn't get out much.''

''Speaking of which.'' Sunni cut in. ''Do you have any friends we can call? Someone who might be worried about you?''

Stephanie filled her daughter's plate, making sure to add some corn, Katie's favorite, and then took a bite of the green beans she'd dished up for herself. ''I guess I'm like your grandmother. I don't get out much—just work and church. I don't really get involved in church, not since...well...'' She glanced at her daughter and changed the subject. ''I know a few people in the business in Baton Rouge that I should contact, I suppose. They're businesses I do contract work for on a regular basis.''

''What do you do?'' Sunni asked.

Stephanie found herself relaxing as she sensed Sunni's genuine interest in her.

''She's into graphic designs and Web pages,'' Ben said, tearing off a piece of roll and popping it in his mouth.

Well, that was close, Stephanie thought, smiling at Ben.

"I also do Internet advertisements, as well as other things," she added.

"Ben, you should get Stephanie to design a Web site for your business," Sunni said excitedly.

"I'm in discussions on that very subject," Ben retorted, grinning.

Ben seemed so easygoing with his sister, allowing her to rattle on, interjecting when he had a chance. He had obviously been very close to his sister growing up.

Sunni was a little older than her brother. The wrinkles around her eyes gave that away. Although she also had smile wrinkles around her mouth, her blue eyes sparkled with fun. Her short brown hair had some gray in it.

She didn't look much like her brother, except for the smile.

"Your husband is offshore?" Stephanie asked, turning the topic from her to Sunni. "Do you work, as well?"

"Oh, no. I'm a full-time mom. I used to work in banking, but I love staying at home," Sunni said proudly.

"That's why I like working out of my

home,'' Stephanie murmured, feeling a sudden connection with the woman.

"Isn't that true. Being at home during the developmental years is so important. It's tight sometimes, but I wouldn't change it for anything in the world.''

Ben chuckled. "I'm not sure how she does it.''

"Oh, you're just too uptight around kids, Ben. You need to learn to loosen up and have fun.''

Stephanie could tell by the look on Ben's face he had no idea how to be fun around kids. "I'll stick with my buildings, thank you, sis.''

Sunni rolled her eyes. "You'd think after six years he would be used to kids. Of course, he works so much he rarely sees my angels.'' Sunni managed to look down her nose at her brother. "I'll break him of that one day.''

Katie giggled.

Stephanie smiled at her daughter, trying to picture Sunni and her brother standing toe to toe as Sunni railed at him for always working. Stephanie couldn't picture it. Ben would tower over Sunni.

She noted Ben was staring at her and lifted

her eyebrow in query. "I'm sorry. Did you say something?"

"Sunni asked you about your house. I said we'd be going over there in the morning. You will feel up to it then, won't you?"

Stephanie nodded. "I'd really like to see what can be salvaged."

"I'll be glad to meet you there. My neighbor can watch my two children, and you'll have an extra pair of hands," Sunni informed her. "And I won't take no for an answer," she said, continuing to smile at her brother. Something in her gaze must have convinced him not to argue because he shrugged and nodded.

After they finished their meal, Stephanie helped clear the table. Sunni shooed her onto the back deck. "Let the children help me. You've had quite a day. We older kids don't bounce back like the younger ones." She winked at Katie, who scampered into the kitchen to help.

Stephanie did as Sunni said, walking onto the redwood deck that stretched a good thirty feet into the hilly backyard. With the sun down, there was a slight breeze rustling the many trees behind the house. It felt good to lean against the wooden rail and feel the peace.

"My sister can be a tyrant."

The sound of Ben's voice, not quite as raspy as earlier today, as he came out through the patio doors, alerted her to his presence.

Smiling into the encroaching darkness, she nodded. "She is definitely a take-charge type of person. Dinner was wonderful."

"Dinner was her idea. Believe me, she's happy to find out all she can. Not that she's a gossip—exactly. She does care, but then, she also likes to be in on everything."

Stephanie chuckled. A small cough escaped.

"How is your throat? You breathed in quite a bit of those fumes."

Ben stopped beside her. He was tall, she realized, and wide. His silhouette blocked out the light coming from the kitchen window. She could smell a light musky aroma emanating from him. She remembered it, vaguely, from when he'd carried her out of the house. He had been strong—and safe.

How she missed that.

Turning to look into the dark night, she said,

"My throat still hurts. Thank heavens I'm around to say that. Thank you, Ben."

His hand touched her chin, pulling her gaze to his. "I think I said earlier we were going to have to have a talk about the thank-yous."

His eyes danced with mischief. His hand felt rough against her chin. She wanted to lean into it, amazingly enough, and feel how it felt against her cheek.

Staring at him, she realized he was very attractive. Embarrassed and glad the night would hide her embarrassment, she replied, "How can I stop saying it?"

She turned her head, and he allowed it, dropping his hand and looking over the wooded area with her. "What if I told you it was an accident? I had decided to start running, to get this body back in shape, and just so happened to run by this morning."

She nodded. "It had to be God."

"What did?" he asked.

"God works in odd ways." She didn't expound on it, not sure how to explain to him that she thought he had been sent by God when he didn't even believe in God.

Puzzlement sounded in his voice as he

asked, "But if it was God, then why didn't He just stop the fire?"

She shrugged. "God may have had a reason for that to happen. We don't understand His ways. It's like we're seeing only a part of the picture, the part that affects our lives. God sees the whole picture."

"You really think God cares? I mean, don't be upset, but I've just never really thought about it. Even if He *could* care, why *would* He care and how would He have time to care about every one of us on such a personal level?"

Stephanie thought carefully before answering. "Well, it says before the world was formed He knew us. So I guess we just have to believe that when Someone loves, Someone who is perfect love, that He cares enough to take a personal interest. Do you know it says He sees every sparrow that falls? And how much more important we are to Him than the sparrows."

Ben shook his head. "What are you talking about?"

Stephanie sighed. "We're getting off the

subject a bit. You asked how I know He cares. It's in the Bible.''

"The sparrow thing, too?'' he asked, not sure.

"Yeah. And many other things. My mom and dad used to read me the Bible when I was little. Didn't your parents read to you?''

Ben shook his head. Clasping his hands in front of him, he admitted, ''My dad split when I was a kid, and shortly after that my mom dumped my sister and me off with my ailing grandma. I was seven at the time, Sunni nine. Grandma raised us.''

Stephanie thought that was awful. "I'm sorry.''

"Don't be. Grandma Betsy worked hard to see we were raised right. She loved us and taught us to be self-sufficient.''

"That's something my parents didn't teach me. When my husband left Katie and me, I wasn't sure we were going to make it. Then I realized that my computer graphics hobby could help me make ends meet. With God's help it all worked out.''

"You put a lot of faith in God, don't you?'' Ben asked curiously.

"I put my whole life in Him," Stephanie replied softly.

"Well! Dishes are loaded, and I'm heading home."

The whirlwind named Sunni strode onto the deck where Stephanie and Ben stood. Behind her trailed her two children. Katie was the only one who was missing. "Your daughter wanted to take another bath and ran off in the direction of the bathroom. My two are getting tired, and I need to get them home. I just wanted to let you know if you need anything to call me. Ben has my number. I'll be glad to help you in any way I can."

Stephanie smiled warmly, thinking how sweet this woman was. "Thank you very much."

"I'm serious," Sunni warned, and went over and hugged her brother. "Call me if you need me. And you," she said, waving a finger at her brother, "you get Stephanie over first thing in the morning so she can get some clothes for her and Katie."

"Yes, ma'am," Ben said sardonically.

With a wave, Sunni turned and headed through the house to the front door.

Stephanie turned to Ben. "I should go find my daughter. She's still too young to be taking baths by herself."

Ben nodded. "You still look worn out. You might want to go ahead and take your evening dose of medication and go back to bed."

Stephanie nodded. "I am still tired. And despite what my energetic daughter thinks, I can tell she's still not feeling well. She usually talks a lot more than this and gets into everything."

Ben chuckled. "She is very well behaved."

Stephanie merely shook her head. "Just wait until she's up to full speed."

Ben nodded, not believing her for one minute. "If you say so."

"Believe me, I do." Nodding, she headed inside to hunt down her daughter. "Thanks, Ben. I'll talk to you in the morning."

"No more thanks!" The words echoed after her.

She couldn't help but smile as she realized that she was driving him silly with her thanks.

"Thank you, God," she whispered as she headed into the bathroom. "Now if You can just make my daughter behave until we get back to our own house."

Chapter Six

*Women may be another species but chil-
dren are from another planet entirely.*
                              —Ben's Laws of Life

Ben dreamed someone had just dropped an anvil on his chest.

He opened his eyes when the anvil moved.

Sitting with legs straddling his chest, staring at him, tears streaming down her face and her thumb in her mouth, five-year-old Katie had made herself right at home.

He'd never had a kid in his room, let alone his bed, let alone his bed when he was in it.

All kinds of horrible thoughts tumbled through his head. "Katie. What are you doing here?" he asked.

Unable to shift his position, he reached up and set her aside, scooting to the far edge of the bed before scrambling out of it. Realizing he only had pajama bottoms on, he started feeling around for a T-shirt.

Katie sniffled.

Pausing in his search, he glanced at her. Seeing the tears filling her eyes he asked, "What is it, honey?" He forgot his fears as concern replaced his bachelor worries.

"I dreamed the house was on fire."

Easing on the bed next to her, he asked, "Your house?"

She shook her head, her thumb still in her mouth.

"This house?"

She nodded, her big brown eyes filling with fresh tears and spilling over.

He patted her shoulder, wondering where her mother was. "Were you looking for your mom?" He thought perhaps she'd gotten rooms mixed up in the dark.

She shook her head. "You saved me," she finally whispered, and crawled into his lap.

He pulled back, stricken to have a little girl sitting on his lap in the middle of the night and in his bedroom.

Katie laid her head against his chest and sniffled again.

What to do?

He didn't want to admit he was freaking out, but... Awkwardly he lifted her until he got her settled comfortably on his hip. He stood and headed toward the hall. "Let's go find Mommie and see what—"

He ran smack into Stephanie, who was tearing down the hall toward the living room at a dead run.

The sound of body meeting body echoed loudly in the stillness of the night...

...just before she bounced back and hit the floor, landing on her bottom, sprawling in the middle of the hall.

She stared up in shock.

He gazed at the woman on the floor, utterly dumbfounded.

"I was coming to find you," he said, continuing to stand there, stunned.

Katie giggled.

Galvanized into action, Stephanie scrambled to her feet. "I was trying to find my daughter. I woke up and was worried—and she wasn't there. I thought maybe she had gotten lost or…"

He realized he still held the child and set her on her feet. He started to reach out to help Stephanie up, recognized it was too late and clasped his hands behind his back awkwardly. "She had a bad dream and ended up in my room."

Her gaze went to his chest.

He crossed his arms as unobtrusively as possible.

"Oh." Obviously nonplussed, she blinked and turned her gaze to her daughter. "Why didn't you come to me, honey?"

"He saved me," Katie whispered.

Nervously Stephanie glanced from Ben to her daughter and back. "I'm so sorry."

Ben glanced at Katie. "Do you think you can sleep now?"

She glanced at his room. "With you?"

"Katie!" Stephanie sounded mortified.

Ben blinked. "Are you still scared?"

Katie nodded.

Ben looked helplessly at Stephanie until an idea formed. "Tell you what. You wait right there."

He went into his bedroom and found the specialty toy his sister had bought him as a gift. After pausing to slip a shirt on, he grabbed the toy and walked to where mother and daughter stood. Ben held a stuffed LSU tiger that wore a purple collar around its neck. He held it out to Katie. "You can sleep with Mike. He'll protect you."

She stared at the tiger, unsure. He reached down and pushed on the tiger's belly, and it let out a loud roar.

Katie's eyes lit up with delight. "He roars!" She accepted it, held the stuffed animal at eye level and stared at it in awe.

Stephanie clasped her hands with worry. "Are you sure it's okay for her to sleep with one of your...toys?"

He flushed. "Sunni gave it to me as a gag gift for my thirty-fifth birthday. She's always giving me things like this. And yes, I'm sure Katie can sleep with it."

"I want to go to bed, Mommie," Katie pronounced, squeezing the tiger again.

Again it roared, and the little girl laughed. As soon as it stopped roaring the child squeezed it again—and again. What had he started?

Stephanie reached out. "Enough, sweetheart. Let's go get you back in bed."

"Can Uncle Ben tuck me in?"

"He's not your uncle, honey," Stephanie said, casting a worried glance at Ben.

"Veronica called him Uncle Ben."

"That's fine if you'd like to call me that, if your mom doesn't mind," Ben offered, his gaze on Stephanie.

Sunni had washed Katie and Stephanie's pajamas, and Stephanie was in hers again. She looked so motherly in the worn pajamas.

When she smiled her okay he found himself relaxing.

"Thank you," she murmured gently, her eyelashes dropping over her eyes as her hands went to her daughter's shoulders. "Would you like to tuck her in?"

Ben paused, wondering if he should. Then

he nodded, thinking that if it would help the child sleep, he'd do it. "Sure."

He followed them into the room and waited until the child crawled into bed. Then, reaching down, he tucked the covers in the side of the bed.

Katie laughed.

So did Stephanie.

"That's not exactly what I meant," Stephanie confided.

Confused, he said, "Sunni always does this with her kids."

"Ah." Stephanie nodded. "Well, I usually just tuck the covers up under her arms and kiss her."

Ben realized Katie was waiting for a good-night kiss. Disconcerted, he leaned down and placed a kiss on the child's forehead. Her skin was so soft and babyish. She smelled of powder.

He had smelled that smell occasionally on Ronnie and Justin. It was definitely one of those foreign scents that made him feel out of place, yet it ignited a small yearning in his heart, too.

Stepping back, he shrugged. "Sleep well."

Katie grinned and hugged the tiger, her teddy bear laying on the table nearby, stained but clean, having been washed with the pajamas before supper—thanks to Sunni.

Ben backed out of the room.

Stephanie leaned over her daughter and kissed her and whispered something. The little girl nodded, and Stephanie said something else before turning to leave. She paused in the hall to turn on the bathroom light and pull the door almost all the way closed. "She was scared of the dark. I hope you don't mind if I leave the light on?"

He shook his head. "Not at all. I guess we should have known she might be frightened after the fire yesterday."

Stephanie nodded. "I was too tired and didn't think."

Ben shifted. "Want some hot tea before you go back to bed?" His throat was hurting, and he imagined hers was too.

"That sounds good," she said.

Silently they headed down the hall and into the kitchen. Ben filled two cups with water and put them in the microwave. While the water heated he grabbed two tea bags, some honey and spoons.

When the microwave beeped, Stephanie retrieved the cups and went to the table.

Ben seated himself and accepted a cup. He added honey, then put an Earl Grey tea bag in and bobbed it in the cup.

Stephanie did the same.

The only light in the room was the one over the kitchen sink. The rest of the house was in darkness. The security light out back caused shadows to seep through the miniblinds by the patio door. The sound of the ceiling fans in the kitchen and living room whisked through the stillness.

"I'm sorry if Katie woke you."

Ben glanced up, surprised. "I was going to apologize for having her in my room. She just showed up."

Stephanie took a sip of tea. Her hair was mussed, like she'd been sleeping really hard and she still had dark circles under her eyes. One cheek had creases on it.

He ran a hand through his hair, figuring it didn't look much better.

"It's your house. No reason to apologize."

Ben shrugged. "I have to admit, I'm not used to kids. Ronnie and Justin only come over with their mom, and they usually go out back to play or watch TV. They've never spent the night and never ended up sitting on top of me in the middle of the night."

"Oh, dear!" Stephanie sounded horrified. Her eyes widened, and her hand covered her mouth.

Ben chuckled. "My reaction exactly when I woke up to find her sitting there."

"I'm so sorry."

"It's okay." He chuckled again. "Actually, now that I'm over my shock I think it's kind of funny. I dreamed someone had dropped an anvil on me. I opened my eyes and there sat Katie, thumb in her mouth staring at me."

Stephanie nibbled her lip. "She only sucks her thumb when she's really nervous or scared."

Ben sobered. "I'm sorry."

Stephanie shook her head. "Don't be. Her dad left when she was nearly three. It hit her hard, and she started sucking her thumb. She hasn't done it for a while now. I guess the dream scared her."

"Does she miss her dad much?"

Stephanie shook her head. "I think...." She sighed. He could see she struggled with her thoughts. He watched her nibble her lip, wrinkle her nose in indecision then sigh again. "He and I didn't have the best relationship. We argued a lot." Looking into her cup, she continued. "He didn't want children, but I didn't know that. I thought everything was fine in our marriage until I got pregnant." She made a face then lifted the cup to take a sip. "Come to find out, he'd had a vasectomy without telling me so I couldn't have children. He was certain I'd cheated on him. That's when the arguments and fights started. All the way through the pregnancy and the birth of Katie we argued. All the way until his girlfriend ended up pregnant, too."

Ben stared, stunned. "Ah..."

"Yeah. He obviously hadn't used protection because he thought his surgery had rendered him safe from accidents—mine *or* his mistress's. When I wouldn't have an abortion, he became furious." Stephanie paused to take another sip of tea.

"He hated kids and he didn't want a fat

wife. According to him, all the women he knew became fat after having kids. He also didn't want some kid interfering in his marriage.'' She sighed then continued. ''It wasn't until Katie was two that I found out about the other woman. It came out during one of our many fights. It seems he'd been having an affair with her for three years. Then he snidely made a comment that she had also been pregnant, but at least she'd handled the problem. She felt the same way he did about kids. I was devastated by his confession. To find out he had a mistress, that he'd gotten her pregnant and had applauded her killing the child was just too much for me to handle all at once. I took Katie and left. I needed to get away from the house for a while so I could reason out what had happened and try to decide how to respond to him. When I returned, he was gone. He'd been gracious enough to leave me a note telling me good riddance.''

Stunned, Ben stared. ''That son of a—''

''Please!'' Stephanie shook her head. ''Don't say it. My husband used to curse all the time, even in front of Katie, and I hated it.''

Ben reddened. "I'm sorry. How could anyone desert their own kid?"

Stephanie shrugged. "He went to church with us on Sunday and Wednesday and was a good lawyer. Everyone respected him. The question boils down to, how could he have fooled everyone the way he did—including me."

Ben didn't know what to say. Still reeling over what Stephanie had told him, he thought someone should track the guy down and beat him within an inch of his life.

"Are you divorced then?"

Bitterly, she nodded. "I never believed in divorce. But one day the papers showed up. My husband had filed and warned me not to contest. He signed over full custody of my daughter. He said if I fought the divorce he'd make sure to get her. Last I heard he and his new wife are living in Europe. Three years and hours and hours of prayers and I think I'm over it…maybe."

"I have no idea where my parents are," Ben confided in the stillness that surrounded them. "And to be honest, other than curiosity, I don't miss them much. My sister and I were very happy at our grandmother's. I'm sure Katie will be okay with you.''

"Okay being raised in a single-parent household?" Stephanie sighed. "That's not how I'd pictured raising a child. The number of children from single-parent households who get into trouble is staggering."

"But you're a stay-at-home mom working to avoid that fate for Katie," Ben said carefully.

"Actually, I'm a charity case staying at your house with nowhere else to go," Stephanie said, correcting him.

"Only for a short time." He reached across the table and squeezed her hand. They both froze, glancing at what he'd just done. Though she was staying in his home, he was really a stranger to her. He removed his hand. An awkward silence ensued, but for some reason he felt as if he knew her a lot better than he did.

Clearing his throat, he finally said, "I've dated some in the past, but nothing was ever serious. Frankly, I didn't have time. I used all of my extra time to build my business." He felt he needed to add that. Actually, he admitted to himself, he didn't date much because he'd never wanted to get serious. There was always that small fear in the back of his mind that if he met a woman and married, she might decide one day to leave—just as Stephanie's husband had left her. He didn't want to risk bringing a child into a world like that. Realizing an awkward silence had fallen, he changed the subject. "I'd like you to consider me for the job of fixing your house. We can discuss it after we see what's left of it."

Stephanie sighed, her gaze drifting over his shoulder. "I don't know if I can afford you or anyone else, Ben. My business provides just enough to make ends meet. As for being able to have enough money for anything over and above the necessities..." Her gaze returned to him.

"You're not getting child support?" Ben asked suspiciously, interrupting her explanation.

She shrugged. "He's in Europe. It's better that he's dead to us than if he were interfering."

Ben nodded his understanding. Who would want a guy like that in her life? "Maybe we could barter," he suggested.

"Like?"

"Well, remember earlier when we talked about our jobs? I told you I needed an advertising campaign? How much would one cost? Perhaps we could make a deal."

"Are you really serious?" Stephanie asked. She finished the mug of tea.

Ben nodded. "If you'd feel more comfortable dealing with John to see I'm on the up-and-up about this, I could arrange that. But our business has really taken off in the last two years. We've been seriously considering putting together an ad campaign for some time now."

Still Stephanie hesitated.

"Don't say no," Ben said. "You just said you're having financial problems. This would be a solution for both of us. And believe it or not, there are still some people that barter occasionally."

He could see her swallowing as if to push down her pride. Then she nodded. "I suppose it wouldn't hurt to discuss it."

"Great," he said. Then he added ruefully, "I hadn't meant to discuss this now. I'd simply meant to tell you that what had happened with your daughter was an accident and that being in the same house, I'm sure things like this are liable to happen.''

''She's not used to having a man around,'' Stephanie said, getting up and tossing the tea bag in the trash can. She put the cup in the sink and added, ''But she seems to have bonded with you because you saved her life.''

Ben sighed and finally accepted it. ''Yeah, I guess I did, didn't I?''

Stephanie nodded and opened her mouth.

''Don't you dare say thank-you again, Annie,'' he warned.

''Stephanie,'' she corrected.

He simply grinned.

She realized what he was doing. ''If I say thank-you you're going to continue with this Annie thing, aren't you?''

His grin widened.

She couldn't help but return his smile. ''Devious,'' she said, feeling freer than she had since the fire.

''Retribution,'' he replied and moved to the sink to dump the contents of his cup and run water in it. He put away the honey and tossed his tea bag in the trash.

She hadn't meant to open up to him so much, but sitting there in the dark with him she'd found him a good listener. And his acceptance of Katie and his teasing...

Oddly enough, she suddenly felt like crying, she was so relieved. Life had been hard the last year, and she was barely making ends meet, but as she'd talked to this man, for a short time she'd forgotten about her problems and been able to enjoy life again.

"Good night," she said, and nodded to him.

"Good night, Annie," he offered wickedly, and headed toward bed.

Her laughter echoed in the dark house.

Chapter Seven

Just when you think you have women and children figured out, you find you don't really know anything at all.
—Ben's Laws of Life

I know what Stephanie told me, but I just don't understand how a man wouldn't want a great child like Katie in his house. Messing up his life, she had said. I'm a bachelor, and if anyone would be put out, it'd be me.

I find Stephanie and Katie wonderful to have around. They don't interfere in the least in my life. As a matter of fact, I learned things from them. The first night had gone well, except for the anvil incident, so I was pretty certain everything would work out.

After all, I'd seen Katie's worst, so everything would be fine and I could settle down to getting to know Stephanie.

Ah, but I was to find out getting to know Stephanie meant getting to know her child, too—and discovering children had many worsts.

The shout woke her.

Followed by the thud.

Something had tipped over.

Jerking up in bed, Stephanie tried to get her bearings.

She was in her neighbor's house—and that darned medicine had made her sleep late!

The clock said seven, and that meant she had to get up, get her daughter ready for school and then go to her house.

But first, she had to find out what that noise was.

Worry that her daughter might be hurt was foremost in her mind.

She shoved back the covers, slipped from bed and hurried from the bedroom.

The room her daughter had slept in was empty.

Oh, dear, she thought, dismayed. Stephanie headed toward the living room.

What met her eyes stopped her in her tracks.

Laying in the middle of the kitchen, cereal surrounding him, was Ben. Her daughter stood on the far side of him, thumb in her mouth, staring at him.

"Katie, are you okay?"

Katie's eyes shot to her mom's, and she nodded but pointed at Ben.

Stephanie's gaze went to the man on the floor wearing nothing except a pair of faded blue jeans.

Brown flakes of cereal and a white filmy substance dotted his torso. A leaking quart of milk lay on the floor nearby. He even had the flakes and milk in his hair.

His gaze was on her, she realized. Weakly, she asked, "Are you okay, too?" She started forward.

He grimaced as if galvanized by her words. "No, don't come forward, and yes, I'll live."

Pushing up, he carefully sat and reached for Katie.

She looked ready to cry.

"It's okay. The milk was just too high for you to reach. It's not your fault. Come here and let me lift you over this mess."

The little girl obeyed.

Any hopes that Ben had made the mess disappeared with his words. Nervously Stephanie flexed her hands and shifted. "I'll clean this up. I overslept. The medication the doctor gave me knocked me out."

The medication and their late-night talk.

Ben shook his head. He looked well rested this morning, even covered in milk and cereal.

As soon as Katie's feet hit the ground she rushed to her mom. "I was getting the milk. He scared me and I dropped everything."

Stephanie took her daughter into her arms and hugged her. "It's okay, sweetheart." She looked to Ben for an explanation.

"The milk was on the top shelf. I came in to fix some tea and saw Katie stretching for it. I, uh, well, startled her when I rushed forward, attempting to ward off exactly what happened."

Stephanie felt her cheeks heat with embarrassment. "I am truly sorry."

Ben shook his head. "I didn't realize my sudden exclamation would scare Katie. Besides, it'll clean up." Looking at himself, he wiped belatedly at his arms, brushing cereal off.

"Please, go wash up and let me clean up the kitchen," Stephanie said.

Ben shook his head. "You're a guest, Stephanie. I can't ask that of you."

"But you'll just make more of a mess."

As if to emphasize her point, she nodded as a flake fell from his hair, bounced off his cheek and tumbled to the floor.

He winced. "Uh, yeah," he admitted. Grinning at Stephanie, he said, "I guess I'll take you up on that offer." He grinned at Katie before meeting Stephanie's worried gaze again. "I'll be off to shower again. When I'm done we can drop off Katie at school and then go look at your house, if you're up to it."

"I'd appreciate that greatly," she replied.

He nodded and headed toward the bedroom. Stephanie turned to her daughter. "Did you get any milk on you?"

Katie shook her head.

"Good. Tell you what, you go get dressed and I'll clean up here and then fix you some breakfast. You can eat while I'm dressing, and then we'll get you to school. Sound good?"

"Can I wear the jeans that Ronnie gave me?"

The glow in Katie's eyes showed the resilience of kids. With a nod Stephanie patted her on the bottom. "Go. And don't forget to brush your teeth."

Her daughter scooted off down the hall while Stephanie turned to clean up the disaster before her. It didn't take her long. She ran a mop she'd found in the pantry over the floor.

She'd noted, except for some papers, pads and pencils lying around, that Ben kept his house immaculate. This was definitely not a house in which children often visited. She'd noted the cleaners under the sink where little hands could reach them and breakables left where children might run into them.

Stephanie didn't totally child proof her house, but certain things she didn't want broken, like possible heirlooms, she kept out of Katie's reach.

He did have a beautiful house, she thought as she finished mopping the shiny floor and went to dress. Even his bedrooms were spacious and open, allowing the early-morning light to shine in.

She would bet he had designed the house, a split-level. The entire house made her feel like she was in the open. Nothing was cramped about the house at all.

She slipped into the slightly too-big jeans and the T-shirt she had borrowed from Sunni, then donned a second short-sleeved shirt. She ran a comb through her hair, brushed her teeth and returned to the living room just in time to see her daughter finishing her bowl of cereal.

Ben came out of the kitchen, tea in hand. ''Want some?'' he asked.

She shook her head. ''Don't want to keep you waiting,'' she said quickly. ''Are you ready, Katie?''

Katie dropped her spoon in the tan and blue ceramic bowl and bounced up.

''In the sink,'' Stephanie warned.

Katie stopped her rush toward the door, hurried back and placed her bowl in the sink. Stephanie crossed and ran some water in it.

By the time she was done, her daughter was already out the door.

"Energetic," Ben murmured, watching Katie skip down the sidewalk to the car.

"Kids bounce back fast," Stephanie agreed.

"Well, then," Ben finally said and motioned toward the door with his mug.

Stephanie took the hint and left, quickly going to the car.

They dropped off Katie with a short explanation about why she had no supplies. Of course, everyone had heard about the fire already, and her teacher was understanding. Stephanie made a mental note to get new supplies for Katie.

Then she and Ben headed to her house before he went to work.

There was no smoke now. From the front it looked perfectly normal, a nice white-painted country home with a long deep porch next to an extended wing where the dining room was located.

But then the driveway curved, giving them a glance at the side of the house. The damage was evident. John had boarded up Katie's room with plywood. Mounds of black charred wood lay not too far away, and a huge blue tarp was tied over the top of the eastern section of the house where the roof had caved in.

''The fire marshal is saying it was electrical. He thinks your drier or hot water heater was the culprit. Both are located where he thinks the fire originated.''

''You talked to the fire department?'' Stephanie asked as they rolled to a stop.

''No. John did. The fire chief was here when John came over to board up the place.'' He exited the car, came around and waited for Stephanie as she climbed out.

She took a few steps forward, then paused to study the damage. She couldn't see much from where she stood, which was both good and bad. Nervousness welled in her gut, eating its way up her throat at the thought of going into her ruined home. There was no telling what she would find. Dealing with this meant facing just how close she'd come to losing everything. But it had to be done. Forcing away the acrid taste of fear, she said, ''I might as well get this over with now.''

Ben reached out, caught her hand and squeezed it. ''Just remember, it can be fixed.''

She nodded. "And my daughter's life was the most important thing," she added.

"Yours, too," Ben gently corrected.

Taking a deep breath, she went forward, Ben at her side. She didn't admit how much this near stranger meant to her now. They were strangers, yet she had formed an attachment that caused her to want him by her side as she went into her house.

He pushed open the door and held out a hand, stopping her from entering. "There still might be some damage. Let me lead."

A feeling of warmth and protection floated through her. It was something she hadn't felt in a long time. For so long she'd been struggling to make ends meet, caring for a child and putting her life back together. She hadn't had time for personal feelings like this.

They felt good.

Taking a deep breath, she allowed those feelings to buoy her as she stepped into the waterlogged house.

It reeked of smoke. Putting her hand to her nose, she squinted against tears. "It smells awful."

Ben went to the back part of the house and

started pulling open drapes, revealing more of the house. It didn't look too bad in the living room, dining room or the kitchen.

However, the walls in the hall were stained and soggy. Squishing sounds filled her ears as she followed Ben down the hall.

"We can get rid of the smoky smell...and the damaged carpet. That'll be one of the first things to go so we can save your floor."

She hadn't thought about the carpet being ruined. She knew her daughter's room and the utility room were damaged, but the smoke smell was everywhere...and the carpet...

As they passed her door, the wall went from sooty to charred black. Near her daughter's room she shivered again. She saw the husk of a room. Debris littered the floor where the fire-fighters had shoved the bed and toys about attempting to put out the fire. Most of the room was gone. Black wood and soggy pieces of cloth—draperies, she thought—along with maybe a blanket and some clothes, were scattered about. Katie's rocking horse was damaged beyond repair, though only the plastic chair of the chalkboard-and-chair set was ruined. The pictures from the wall were cracked, lying on the floor or missing completely. On the south side of the room, however, Stephanie found the chest that held her daughter's clothes in one piece, though wet. The closet was okay, too. The pictures on that side of the wall were still intact, one of a lamb, another of Jesus and children gathered around and a drawing of Katie's that she'd framed. They wouldn't be salvageable however, because they were saturated with water.

The eerie blue of the tarp shaded the room from the elements. The tarp snapped loudly as a gust of wind caught it and tried to work its way beneath it. Glancing at the blue plastic, she thought how her outlook had changed in such a short period of time. Some things had seemed important before... Now, after all that had happened, she realized her daughter's safety mattered more than the clothes she wore or the now ruined chest she had so painstakingly varnished. She and her daughter were alive. That was what was important.

"The room is pretty sound. You can tell the fire came from north, in the utility room, which is completely gone. Still, it'll take a couple of weeks to rebuild this part of the house."

"Two weeks?" She was shocked to reality. Her gaze shot to Ben's. "I can't stay with you two weeks."

"Gee, thanks," he murmured and chuckled.

Flushing, she clasped her hands, embarrassed. He had helped her so much already. She knew he wouldn't be able to stand having strangers that long in the house. "I didn't mean..."

"I know exactly what you meant." He cut in, not seeming the least bit bothered by her words. "It'll take a week to clean up the area enough that you can move back in. We're going to have to paint the entire inside of the house to get rid of the burned smell. And we'll go ahead and pull up the carpet in the living room, as well. You can move in before we put the new carpet down, while we're working on the other room. But the electrician will have to come out first...and your insurance adjuster."

"I see," Stephanie said, trying to picture the plan he was laying out on the canvas of her mind.

"Please, Stephanie, don't worry about where you're going to stay. Just accept it as the neighborly thing to do and work on my advertising project while I work on your house.''

She strode slowly out of the room and down the hall to her bedroom. She went in and looked around. She heard Ben behind her. ''It looks like my room came through unscathed. All of my equipment is okay. It's dry.'' She stomped on the floor with her foot.

''Your door blocked most of the spray that came down the hall.''

She glanced at the hall where Ben stood and noted that it was wet. ''I suppose my washer and drier and water heater are shot?''

Ben nodded. ''You could say that. We might be able to set you up with some used ones.''

She flushed, realizing he knew she was worried about money.

''Or your insurance might cover new ones if you'd rather.''

She thought she'd rather have used and save what she could, but then again... Her old washer had been about to break down anyway. ''This is all so much to take in.''

His forehead creased into a small frown as he crossed the room. His strides were long and quick as he closed the distance between them.

Before she knew what he was about, he reached up and clasped her shoulders. He squeezed them gently and simply held her.

The warmth of the long, curved hands providing support and understanding was her undoing.

Stephanie shuddered, and a sob escaped.

Mortified, she tried to pull away, not understanding why she felt like the floodgates of the Hoover Dam had suddenly opened.

Ben wouldn't let her. He wrapped his large arms around her and pulled her firmly to him. ''This has been coming for a long time. Go ahead and let it out.''

She didn't understand what he meant, but his words had the desired effect. Her arms went around him, gripping him to keep herself from sliding into a puddle at his feet. She started crying. They weren't pretty, gentle tears to catch a man's eye, or tears of frustration or anger. These were tears that could be likened to a volcano that had finally erupted. Soul-cleansing tears that had built up for three years. Tears that brought back the memories of inadequacy when her husband had left her and the feelings of guilt for the pregnancy that had resulted in her beautiful daughter. These were tears for the many days she had been so angry at her daughter as she'd tried to care for her, tears because of the many sleepless nights she'd spent trying to do all the chores that needed to be done to keep her daughter happy, healthy and with a roof over her head.

The house burning down was the final injustice. Despite how hard she had tried, things had not worked out. She had failed. Belatedly she realized she heard the beeping of a pager. It wasn't hers. It must be Ben's. But she couldn't stop crying.

Amidst it all she heard a female voice in the background tsking, then other arms went around her. She heard Ben murmur, missed his arms but clung to the new person who had come in as she continued to cry.

And slowly those tears of helplessness changed to tears of relief. So she had failed in many ways, she thought as the tears continued to flow. But she hadn't given up. And God was still in control. Look at the chance she had to have her house fixed in exchange for doing an ad campaign. The house had needed some work, she thought as the tears slowed. This would be a way to see it done...and she knew God had better plans in store for her. Things would work out.

Perhaps she could wash away those old feelings of guilt, frustration and anger and at last start anew. Just as the new paint applied to her house would be fresh, this could be an opportunity to make a new beginning in her life. The only thing she and her daughter really needed to be happy was God and each other. All the other things she'd been so angry about and the material things she'd been unable to give her daughter, weren't really necessary. She could make it. A verse from the Bible came to mind about God's peace being given to us. She felt the indwelling of the Holy Spirit touch her and begin to heal her heart, a healing she hadn't been able to accept for three years now.

She realized that her Shepherd did indeed take care of every sheep He had, including this one who had just fallen apart in front of near strangers.

Silently she whispered a prayer of thanks to God. She was leaning on Sunni's strong shoulder while listening to the sweet, gentle voice inside her.

"Are you ready to talk yet? It's okay, honey. It really is."

The first words Stephanie could make out as she finally calmed were those words from Sunni. Looking at the woman who had somehow managed to get her to sit down on the bed, she saw Sunni's concerned face staring at her.

What could she say to Sunni?

With a shuddering sigh of peace she finally said, "Isn't God good?"

Chapter Eight

❧

*Just when you think you have life figured
out, a woman changes your mind.*
                                    —Ben's Laws of Life

"Is she okay?"

Sunni brushed a stray strand of hair from her
face and seated herself directly across from
Ben. "She's fine. We had a long talk."

"Was she upset about me leaving? I mean
I just left her... Did she miss me?" Ben set
the phone down and shoved the papers he had
been working on to the side before leaning forward, forearms propped on his desk.

He'd worried about leaving Stephanie, but she hadn't seemed to notice. His sister had come in and taken charge of her. Nor did she seem to notice when he'd said he had an emergency and had to go. Someone had robbed their storage warehouse last night, and he had to make a report.

He'd felt like a heel for the last two hours as he'd tried to get hold of his sister and at the same time attempted to sort through the inventory paperwork.

Sunni shifted in her seat, glancing out to where John stood chatting with Stephanie. Ben noted the way John reached out and took Stephanie's elbow, all charm as he pointed toward the work site and motioned as if to take her on a tour.

She evidently accepted, for he called to one of the men who came over and passed her a hard hat.

Ben frowned.

"I think she was."

"Was what?" Ben glanced at his sister and saw she had an odd look on her face—just before she burst out laughing.

"You asked me if she missed you. I said I

thought she did. She didn't say anything, mind you,'' Sunni continued in amused tones. He wondered if she realized she'd answered a question that had flitted into his mind. ''She didn't say anything at first, that is.''

Here we go, Ben thought, exasperated. His sister wanted to tell everything and drag the story out syllable by syllable. That really got to him, and Sunni knew it. She absolutely reveled in his misery, and she would make him work for every word. ''So what did she say at first?'' he asked, gearing himself up for the ordeal.

Sunni frowned. ''She has the strangest relationship with God.''

Of all the things Ben had expected to hear, that wasn't it. The patience he had started to gear himself up for fled. ''Go on,'' he encouraged, totally perplexed as to what his sister could mean.

''I mean, her first words were, 'Isn't God good?'''

That really wasn't what he'd expected. ''Come again?'' Stunned, he stared at his sister. Good? His sister had to have heard Stephanie wrong.

"I'm serious, Ben. When she was done crying she looked at me and said, 'Isn't God good?' I swear I was as stunned as you are. But…"

She paused and frowned, her gaze unfocused as if she were looking inward.

"But?" he asked, forcing himself not to reach across the table and shake the words out of her.

"Well, I have to admit, for someone who'd just seen their house destroyed and probably lost just about everything, she had a peaceful look on her face when she said that."

Ben didn't get it. Staring at his sister, he tried to understand but he couldn't. No longer in a hurry to hear the story, he tried to make sense of what his sister said. "She was crying her heart out when I left, Sunni. How could she look peaceful?" He remembered her red splotchy face as she'd sobbed like her heart couldn't be mended, her gasping breaths, the way she heaved, looking like a fragile, broken porcelain figurine he couldn't put back together again. They had shaken him, those deep, soul-wrenching sobs—shaken him more than he cared to admit.

Sunni waved a hand, her gaze focusing on her brother. ''It was the strangest thing. I asked her the same thing about that peaceful look, and she actually chuckled, though it sounded a bit watery, if you know what I mean.''

He didn't, but he wasn't going to ask. His sister was finally talking, and if he didn't interrupt he might hear the rest of the story before John carried Stephanie off to Outer Mongolia.

''At any rate, she went on to say that God wasn't the one who caused the fire, but God could certainly use it to His glory.''

''Huh?'' Confused, Ben had to wonder just what he'd gotten himself into. This woman sounded like she was talking an entirely different language.

''It's hard to explain,'' Sunni said and clasped her hands in her lap.

It must be really hard to explain, Ben thought, if Sunni wasn't going to animate the entire thing as she talked.

''You see, according to her, there were problems with the house that the fire destroyed, like needing a new room in that spot and a new washer and drier. And though it destroyed some of the house, her insurance will pay for those things...and she'll get them fixed without having to put out the money herself.''

He stared at his sister, thinking in an odd way that made sense. He would never have thought of it that way, nor would he consider it a blessing to have his house burn down. But... "How is that for...what'd you say? God's glory?'' He got up, crossed the room and poured himself a cup of coffee before glancing out the window in the direction in which John and Stephanie had headed.

''Well, she said that Christians should be able to praise God in whatever circumstances they were in. Whether they were good or bad, whether they were happy or sad, they should still be able to tell God how happy they are and be able to see the good in the situation and see God working in it.''

''I suppose that's one way to look at it,'' he muttered and lifted his coffee to take a drink.

''She thinks you are sent by God, too.''

He nearly choked. He jerked the cup forward, then jumped back to miss the spilling liquid. Glancing at his sister, he said, ''I don't even go to church. How in the Sam Hill did she come up with that?''

Sunni chuckled, obviously pleased with his reaction. He shot her a withering look, returned to his desk, set the cup down and started to clean up the mess.

''She said that you were running by the house at the right time and that you heeded something inside you that told you to check on them. You also offered to repair her home if she'd do an ad campaign for you...which was a blessing to her, because she doesn't have much money. She said something so coincidental had to be the work of God.''

He shook his head. ''I'm God's handyman, then, am I?'' Forgetting the coffee, he dropped to his chair, incredulous at what Sunni had just told him.

Sunni waved a hand at him. ''Oh, stop it. I found her story fascinating. She really has a strong faith. Do you know, she believes that God loves each person so much He's actually there to talk to that person if he or she calls His name?''

Ben couldn't imagine anyone believing that. But then, he'd never been big on church, nor had he really known many churchgoing people. Come to think of it, he really had no idea what a Christian believed. The two or three people he knew who said they were Christians didn't talk to God. He was some specter who encompassed everything like the earth and good and stuff. "She thinks of God as talking to people? I'm sure, if that were the case, we'd know something about that," Ben said dryly.

Sunni rolled her eyes. "You are really impossible, Ben. I'm serious. She said it's an internal prompting, a small voice telling you not to do or to do something, the Word of God as you read it telling you something in your heart. She said that's God talking to you."

"I get those feelings but I don't go to church," he objected.

She shrugged. "She said it's God's Spirit Who is everywhere that does that. When I asked about the bad things people do, she said that it's not God's Spirit prompting them but another one altogether."

He wasn't sure about any of this, though it did make him curious. At least he knew a bit more about Stephanie. He couldn't help but admit the woman fascinated him, though this last bit was going to take some digestion.

"After she told me that she asked where you were."

Ben glanced up sharply. His sister sounded way too casual when she said that. She also had that I'm-not-interfering look on her face, which meant just the opposite. "And you told her?"

She shrugged. "I said you had an emergency."

"Oh?" he asked, not believing that Sunni could explain something to someone in only one sentence.

"She was really worried about the break-in, but that was after I saw disappointment on her face. I think she had really wanted to talk to you and tell you everything she told me. She was at peace, she said, and I think she wanted you to know that, for some reason."

"She was disappointed I wasn't there?" He couldn't help but zero in on that. How odd, he thought, although he did like knowing that she seemed to miss him.

Sunni grinned, and he realized immediately his mistake.

"You like her, don't you? I knew it! I knew from the moment you didn't call me that you must have felt something for her—"

"I had just gotten home—"

"—and you just couldn't put it into words. Oh, Ben, this is wonderful. Stephanie is so sweet. I really like her and think she'd make a wonderful sister-in—"

"Stop right there!" The near roar got his sister's attention. But not like he wanted. She grinned and ducked her head in mock humility.

"I won't say another word," she promised.

Yeah, right, he thought disbelievingly. "I don't even know this woman. I just helped her and her kid out. They needed the aid, and I helped them, Sunni. That's it." Defensively he set his jaw and waited for her response. It wasn't long in coming.

"Of course that is the only reason, Ben," Sunni said. Ben scowled to show his disgruntlement at her smarmy attitude.

Before he could say anything, however, the door opened, and John and Stephanie walked in.

Ben glanced immediately at Stephanie. She looked good standing there in his office. The hard hat was gone, her hair a bit wild from the wind, which had whipped it out of her clip, but he liked that look. Out of the corner of his eye he saw Sunni looking like the cat who'd eaten the canary, sitting there grinning. Giving a warning glance toward his sister, he stood and went around his desk.

"How'd the tour go?" he asked.

"Are we interrupting?" John queried, studying the look on Sunni's face.

Ben shook his head. "No. Sunni was just leaving."

"Oh," Stephanie said, her eyes going wide as she glanced from one person to another. She pushed one of the stray strands of hair back, leaving her high cheekbone clear. Ben noticed the color the wind had added to her face. "I came to see if I could get a more thorough look at your operation and see what it was all about and possibly ask you some questions about what you might want as a workup..."

"You can stay."

Ben said that a bit too bluntly. The room went quiet. Stephanie shifted. Her gaze went to Sunni before uncomfortably shifting to John. She avoided looking at Ben.

"Sunni brought me here," she finally said.

Great, Ben, just great, he thought. Of course Sunni had brought her there. "I'll be glad to take you home whenever you're done." Her gaze shot to his. Electricity shivered down

Ben's back as they stared at each other. He cleared his throat and added, "John is in charge today. I'm just doing paperwork." He waved a hand toward the work area. "I can assign someone to show you around and then we can go out to lunch, discuss what I want for a workup, and then I can drop you off so you can pick up your car."

Stephanie hesitated, then a slow smile of acknowledgment creased her face. "That'd be nice, Mr...."

"Just Ben."

"Just Ben," she corrected quietly, that small smile still playing about her lips.

"Well, I'll be off then," Sunni called, interrupting the rapport between Ben and Stephanie. Glancing around the room, finally acknowledging there were other people there, he saw John gaping at him.

"And you can escort me out," Sunni said to John, and hooked his arm before he could comment. "Don't forget to wipe up your mess," she called.

"I'll be back in a minute," John said as Sunni pulled him toward the door.

Confusion on her face, Stephanie watched

them go. After the door was closed, she turned to Ben and asked, ''What was that all about?''

Ben rolled his eyes. There was no way he was going to tell her what that really was all about. Forcing himself under control and to get his mind back on business, he said, ''My sister is certifiable. She really is. You'll get used to it, though.'' Motioning to a chair, he said, ''Have a seat and we'll get started.'' Quickly he crossed to the coffee table and grabbed a paper towel from the holder next to the sugar bowl. Going to the place he'd spilled the coffee, he squatted and cleaned up the remains.

When Ben finished, he seated himself behind the desk, calling on the nearby radio for one of his men to report to the office. As he talked to Rayford, he had to wonder if lunch with Stephanie would be a mistake.

It was business, after all. His sister was crazy to think there was anything going on between them. Stephanie was just a woman in need of help.

That was it.

Chapter Nine

*Asking a woman a question opens you
up to the dangers of having to listen.*
                                    —Ben's Laws of Life

He was taking her out for lunch.

Was something up here?

Had he read her interest in him?

Seeing him behind the desk, his sleeves
pushed up, the papers surrounding him, that
look on his face as she'd walked in, she had
suddenly realized how very attractive the man
was, and how available.

She'd gulped in stunned shock to discover she actually felt a stirring of desire for the man.

She barely knew him. How could she be attracted to him?

He'd been acting odd, but then had invited her out to lunch.

Maybe that was it. Maybe he had noticed how she'd reacted to him and he was taking her to lunch to let her down easily.

Oh, what was she thinking? Frustrated, she forced herself to admit she was a divorced single parent. She wasn't what a bachelor would be looking for. Besides, since she did have a child, he wouldn't be looking for signals from her that she might be interested! And she wasn't interested in someone who wasn't a devout Christian. She didn't want another man like her husband, who had never read his Bible, never prayed and had gone to church as a social thing. If she'd known then what she knew now...

She was certain she wasn't interested.

No way, no how.

''Ever eaten at Mi Casa's?''

She glanced at Ben and realized he had

stopped in front of a Mexican restaurant in Baton Rouge. Get hold of yourself. She mentally berated herself. "No. No, I haven't. But I do like Mexican food." As she'd told him in the office, just before Rayford had shown up to give her a more detailed look at the company's business plan.

She'd been gone an hour before getting back, and Ben had immediately put his papers aside and whisked her off for an early lunch.

Ben slipped out of the driver's seat and from the car. Starting to follow, she found herself stuck. The seat belt wouldn't budge. Fighting with the seat belt in embarrassment, she was surprised when Ben opened the door. Glancing up, she said, "The seat belt—" click "—was stuck."

Her cheeks were flushed.

He grinned, flashing her a winning smile. "I'm old-fashioned anyway. I like to open the door for women. But women today are too fast on the door handle."

At his chuckle she felt the tension over the situation dissolve. She swung her feet out and allowed him to help her, then he closed the door behind her.

Amazingly, she felt like a queen after such a minor courtesy. They entered the restaurant together and were seated in the back, away from the kitchen, in a quiet little corner.

The waitress handed them menus and took their drink order. As she left, Ben said, "So tell me a bit about your work and how you got started."

Relieved to talk about something she knew, Stephanie said, "I have always enjoyed working with computers. A friend of mine at church knew of my interest. Her husband owns a business, and they were looking for someone to work up print and billboard ads for them. Bill and Amy had an idea what they wanted. She asked me if I knew of anyone who might be interested in the job. I didn't," Stephanie said, and nodded to the waitress, who had returned with tea, chips and salsa.

"Ready to order?"

Stephanie glanced at the menu. "Taco salad," she replied, and waited while Ben placed his order.

"Number two," he said, indicating a lunch special of enchiladas.

The waitress smiled and left.

"And since you didn't know anyone?" Ben asked before picking up a chip to snack on.

Stephanie chose one and played with it, tapping it to knock off the extra salt. "I started working up what she wanted on the computer. You know, we were just chatting, I was in front of the computer...and I said, something like this as I worked and she was so amazed she asked me if I'd be interested in the job."

"And you said yes," Ben concluded.

Stephanie shook her head. "I said no."

At Ben's surprise, she continued. "I had never done anything like that. I wasn't sure what I was doing. Sure, I did Web pages and built sites for different groups I belonged to, including the church and even my husband's practice. But to do the work as a business?" Stephanie shook her head. "I told Amy to give me three days and I'd get back to her. I thought I might come up with some ideas she could use."

"So you did take the job?" Ben asked.

Stephanie chuckled. "Not exactly. I worked up what she had wanted, coming at the idea from different angles with different types of artwork. I went to a store and found supplies and printed up everything and then presented it to her and Bill after service on a Wednesday night. They loved it.''

Ben nodded, though he looked thoroughly confused. ''So they were your first client?''

''Yes. Even though I had expected them to take the work to someone, they really wanted me to do the work for them. However, since I wasn't sure it would work for what they wanted, I told them I had done it for free.''

His eyes widening, Ben said, ''That's not a way to build a business.''

''Au contraire, mon ami,'' Stephanie said, laughing. ''Bill's campaign was very successful and helped increase their profits. Amy convinced me to go into this part-time, and they started referring all kinds of people my way. Some were willing to take a chance on a mother who worked out of her house, some weren't. However, my clientele has slowly increased, and I estimate in another two years I'll make enough to live comfortably.''

''Bill and Amy sound like really good friends.''

Stephanie smiled, though she felt her smile contract a bit. ''They were. Bill had a heart attack last year and died. Amy sold the business and moved back to Oregon to be near her family.''

''I'm sorry.''

Stephanie shook her head. ''Don't be. Bill was a Christian.''

At her statement Ben cocked his head. ''What does that have to do with her missing her husband?'' Somehow he didn't understand how being a Christian would lessen the woman's pain.

Stephanie glanced at her lap, a bit nervously, he thought. Then she glanced up. ''Christians believe that if you have come to the realization of being a sinner and invite Christ into your heart to be Lord of your life, that you start a new life from that day forward, a better life.''

He'd heard terms like that before but didn't understand what they meant. Especially the way Stephanie was phrasing it. ''Yeah. You go to church and stuff,'' he added a bit lamely, still not sure how this had anything to do with death.

She shook her head. ''I'm not explaining it well. What it means for Amy and her husband is that Bill is so much happier now. What he has been striving for has happened. His death was simply a transition, so to speak, a new life with Christ, in heaven, where there is no more pain or tears. He's with his Heavenly Father now. You see, one thing that really bothered Bill was he never knew his father. When he asked Jesus into his heart he used to tell people he might not have an earthly father, but he had a Heavenly Father he could talk to all the time.''

That jolted Ben. He didn't have a father, either. He knew what it was like not to have a father or a mother—to be on your own.

She was basically saying that this man considered God his father and talked with Him. Interesting.

Still curious, he said, as casually as possible, ''Sunni said you think that your house burning down was God's will.''

''No, no, no,'' Stephanie said, shaking her head, smiling.

She took a sip of water, then smiled at him. ''God doesn't do things like that to His children.''

''Children,'' Ben murmured.

She smiled. ''God has one Son, but many

children. We're all his sons and daughters—those who accept that He came to earth to die for our sins. It's so easy to understand when you have a child. I love my child more than life itself. I would never do anything to hurt her. Occasionally I allow certain things to happen so that she can learn from them. God is the same way with us. There is an entire world going on beyond our view, a spiritual world, with good and evil working, fighting for our souls, for our lives. Things happen in this world, things we sometimes can't understand.''

''Like your electrical fire?'' Ben asked.

She nodded. ''Exactly. I don't know why it happened, but I can tell you I had been praying for a new roof and a solution to my financial problems. And I truly believe in an odd way that God is using this to fulfill that prayer. After all, look what is going to be replaced because of the fire. In other words, bad things can be used for our good.''

He found himself grinning in response to her optimistic smile. She was right. She was getting a new roof out of it, plus a few new appliances and a new room....

He shook his head in utter amazement. He didn't think he'd ever seen anyone who could be so positive about something that had been so awful. "It's all a bit odd, if you ask me. I really don't understand much of what you say."

Stephanie took a breath, as if fortifying herself, and said, "Why don't you come to church with me, meet some of the people and listen to our pastor? Maybe he can explain it better than me."

Cocking his head, he asked, "Why do you do that?"

Stephanie blinked. "Do what?"

"Every time anyone has brought up God, you seem to brace yourself, or maybe you're nervous. I'm not sure."

He felt as if he were peeling an onion. Layer after layer of this woman he didn't understand had to be removed before he could find the real her.

She flushed a bright red, and her eyes darkened with shame. "I'm sorry. I didn't realize it was so obvious. It's just in the world today people aren't very accepting of Christianity."

He had to disagree with her there. "I don't

see that at all. Most everyone I know is…well, they don't care if someone goes to church or believes in God.''

Slowly, she shook her head. ''That's not Christianity, Ben.''

He was confused. And she obviously saw it because she spread her hand on the table. ''Believing in God doesn't make one a Christian.''

''Then what does?'' He was plain lost now.

''Being a Christian means coming to the realization that you are a sinner, that even if it was only me that had sinned in this world that Christ would have still come for me. But as we know, the Bible tells us all have sinned and come short of the glory of God. That means we've all strayed from the path God set for us. Each and every one of us. We realize this and realize that our life just can't go anywhere without Him because we were created to worship Him. You see, we are made up of three parts, Ben, body, soul and spirit. Our body houses our intellect or soul, but our spirit is empty because our sin separated us from God. We try to find things to fill that emptiness, whether it is entertainment, social activities,

work, love or even sex. Everyone tries to find
that perfect life.''

''What's the matter with that?'' He wondered if he'd broken one of his own rules,
which was don't ask a woman a question unless you knew something about the subject.
But still, he couldn't help but wonder about
this relationship thing she had spoken to Sunni
about. ''Don't you want to be happy?
Shouldn't you strive for that?''

She smiled a soft smile that made him forget
his prickliness over her comment. ''Of course
you do, Ben. But true happiness can't be found
until you find peace with Jesus Christ. You
can't really understand love until you understand what Love did for you. When we submit
to Him and accept that He sent His son to die
for our sins so we can be reconciled to Him,
then...*then* we can experience true happiness.''

The food arrived.

Ben had never been so thankful in his life
to see a waitress. He felt really odd listening
to Stephanie. It was a feeling he didn't know
how to explain, but it had been like a vise gripping his chest as she'd talked. He'd only un-

derstood about half of what she tried to tell him.

He was simply glad that that discussion was over.

The conversation resumed as Stephanie started poking at her salad and talking about her daughter. "Katie loves black olives. She won't eat them, mind you, but she insists they come on her food if we go out so she can make a face with them." Stephanie laughed then bowed her head and said a silent prayer.

Ben shifted, and for the first time in his life said silently, *Thank you for the food, God,* wondering if God would really hear him. He felt it was the least he could do after telling Stephanie that most people believed in God. He believed in God, too. He just never realized there was any more to the Christianity thing than that.

But evidently with Stephanie there was much more to it. And strangely enough, now that she had changed the subject, a million and one questions flooded his mind, questions about what she had said, what she had meant and what it all might mean to him.

As they started eating he realized that he

might just find some answers if he took her up on her offer. If he went with her Sunday, maybe the pastor at her church might have some answers.

He wasn't sure if he wanted to go or not. He still had time to decide.

It was going to be a long week.

Chapter Ten

Sometimes experience is the only way to understand a woman and life.

> —Ben's Laws of Life

On Sunday morning, Stephanie thought things were going very well, considering...

Until she walked into the living room, dressed in a skirt and top for church, and found Ben wearing a drop-dead gorgeous casual suit—and looking wonderful.

She had stood gawking until he'd offered to go change. Realizing she was making a fool out of herself and embarrassing him, she told him he was dressed perfectly. And he was.

Once they arrived at the church, she'd registered Katie in children's church, which had surprised Ben, as he had no idea they had special services for children. Then they'd entered the church's foyer. It was an attractive small area with light-blue carpet and painted walls. A small table to their left held bulletins and a pink floral arrangement.

Ben took a bulletin and headed toward the double doors that led into the sanctuary. He accepted the monthly magazine that one of the ushers handed him. Jason, a young single adult who stood near the front door chatting with different people as they passed, surprised Ben when he stopped him and welcomed him to the service.

This was a friendly church, though after Bill had died and Amy had left, Stephanie hadn't taken time to get to know many people. Being married and then single did put her at a disadvantage. After all, most of the married couples liked to socialize with other couples, and she was no longer a couple.

''I like to be close so I can see and not be distracted if some of the teenagers or others start talking.'' Stephanie pointed to the third row.

Ben cocked his head, and Stephanie again noticed how good he looked this morning and how good he smelled as his musky cologne drifted her way.

''People *talk* during the service?''

''Do you know a teenager who could ever... Oh, never mind,'' she said, chuckling. ''I forgot you don't really know any kids.''

He turned the bulletin over in his hand again, and she realized teasing him about being a bachelor might not be wise. Sunni might do that, but Stephanie really was just a neighbor, though she felt she had gotten to know him this past week. She'd be in her own home soon and she would be glad because she'd definitely found she liked chatting with Ben too much. Seated, she could feel the warmth next to her from his body heat. She remembered the days when she had someone sitting next to her, the feeling of closeness and of not being alone. It was nice to have an adult standing by her as she stood to sing.

Several people stopped and shook their

hands on the way to their seats before church started.

As the service began, Stephanie raised her hands in the air and gave herself up to the worship service, praising God and finding a beautiful release in her spirit over the worries of the past week.

Eventually the song service ended, they were seated and her pastor, Robert, a short round man who really knew his stuff, stood up to preach.

She noted the look of surprise on Ben's face as Pastor Robert started speaking. That was the only emotion she noted, however, as the service continued. Robert's message was on trusting God. Surprised and pleased, Stephanie settled in to listen, hoping what Pastor Robert said helped Ben understand more of what she had tried to explain the other day.

Then the service was over. Robert gave an altar call, people sang as others went up for prayer. People finally started leaving. Ben was surprised when Stephanie stopped by a table and picked up a Bible and handed it to him. ''If you don't have one, these are free,'' she said.

Ben ran his hand over the front before tucking the book under his arm. She was right. Though he'd thumbed through a Bible once or twice in hotel rooms, he didn't own one, nor had he ever really read one. He remembered a huge fancy one his grandma had owned. It had had a bunch of names in the front of it. He'd never seen his grandmother open it except to share names with them from that first page. It felt different to have one that was his.

Many people stood in groups chatting and laughing. Others hurried toward their cars. Stephanie went to get Katie.

Ben followed Stephanie. The service had certainly been an experience he hadn't expected, he thought as they walked to the building where the kids met for service. He'd seen television scenes with people walking down the aisles in fancy robes carrying candles and stuff—but that hadn't happened here. There were no opera-sounding songs and deep, slow voices.

The whole experience was different than he thought it would be. Especially as he watched kids run everywhere. Ben stood by as Stephanie presented a number and Sunday school teachers called for Katie. The children were watching an animated movie with a boat...he realized it must be the story of Noah's Ark.

Stephanie, her skirt clinging to her body, was very lovely this morning. She had always looked like a mom to him until today. She was drop-dead beautiful with her hair pulled back in a French braid, a dark skirt and shiny tan top. She had tiny ankles and wore old-fashioned heels on her feet, not the current clunky type but dainty ones. Probably because she didn't have money to spend on things like dress shoes, he realized, but they looked perfect on her, at any rate.

"Are you ready to go?" Stephanie asked as her daughter ran up to her.

"Yep!" Katie said, her brown curls bouncing as she screeched to a halt in front of her mom. "It was so much fun today, Mommie. We learned about Noah and being left behind and how many animals went on the boat and that we need to be ready for Jesus."

Stephanie bent and hugged her daughter. Seeing it, Ben felt a yearning in him that was unfamiliar. He was feeling an emotional overload—first the service and now this. Too many things to think about and to sort out.

"Sounds like fun, Katie. Guess what? Sunni invited us over for dinner today. Do you want to go?"

Katie looked at Ben. He immediately devoted his attention to her. "Will Ronnie and Justin be there?"

Ben nodded and offered her a grin. "They sure will."

"Yeah!"

Stephanie laughed.

Ben chuckled. The interaction between mother and daughter was a wonderful thing to watch. It helped him find something to concentrate on instead of the service. It hadn't been what he had expected at all, but then, that was becoming his mantra, he thought.

"Shall we go, ladies?" he asked and motioned toward the parking lot.

Katie giggled and ran toward the car.

Stephanie gave him a sweet smile that warmed his gut and made him forget about everything but her. "She really likes you."

He found himself smiling back. "I like her, too—I think."

Stephanie laughed outright. "I can't believe kids are so foreign to you, with Veronica and Justin in your family."

He shrugged. Touching her elbow, he started toward the car. "I've never really had time for them."

Stephanie's smile dimmed. "Kids are something special. You've got a wonderful niece and nephew there."

He nodded. "Yes, I do."

They arrived at the vehicle, and he opened the door for Stephanie. Katie was already strapped in the back seat waiting to go.

When Stephanie was inside he walked around to the driver's side and climbed in.

"You said she lives in Slaughter?"

He nodded. "About ten minutes from here. In the old section, not too far from the main post office."

"Is there anything else out there?" Stephanie asked, and chuckled.

Ben joined her. "The outlying areas are farms and such. They're included in the population of the town. It's a shame that there are only two or three businesses in Slaughter."

"At least the town is still there. Probably

because of the Civil War battles that took place there."

Ben shrugged. "Or the fact that the Co-op is there. People live just far enough away from Baton Rouge and Zachary to feel like they're in the country, but not far enough away for it to be inconvenient."

"I think you hit on it," Stephanie agreed.

"Have you ever lived in a town that small?" he asked as they left the parking lot and started down Plank Road toward Slaughter.

Stephanie shook her head. "Except for Pride."

Ben chuckled. "Yeah, but Pride isn't really considered an official town."

"I go to school in Pride." Katie piped up from the back.

Ben grinned, glancing in the mirror to note that Katie was drawing on a paper she had brought out of the children's service. "That's true," he agreed.

"Pride's population is less than Slaughter. I wonder if it will ever get as big as Slaughter, if it'll have police or town officials," Stephanie mused.

Ben nodded. "If it incorporates. You know,

Pride got its name from the town's postmaster. It's said that the town was called Sandy Creek because of a small creek in the area, but when they went to put a post office in, the postmaster's wife said they should call it Pride.''

Stephanie's eyebrows inched up. ''Really? I had no idea.''

Ben grinned. He liked to see the surprise on Stephanie's face. ''And Slaughter is named after a family that lived there, not Slaughter Field, where the Civil War battle took place.''

''I had wondered how a town would come up with a name like Slaughter. How about Zachary?'' she asked.

''You got me there,'' Ben said as he turned onto a side road that would lead them into Slaughter. ''Maybe because Zachary Taylor was originally from this area?''

''Really?''

Ben glanced at Stephanie. ''You didn't know?''

She shook her head.

''He helped build some barracks in downtown Baton Rouge. I'll have to take you on a tour.'' He grinned.

She grinned back. ''It's a date.''

Those words caused his stomach to clench with anticipation. Stephanie froze, her eyes widening.

He realized she hadn't thought before she'd said those words, but he couldn't stop his response. His eyes darkened. "Is that a promise?" he asked, his voice coming out rougher than he meant.

She swallowed. "I—well, I meant…"

He had to turn his gaze away to make a turn onto a different street. When he glanced back, she had regained her composure. Her hands were folded in her lap and she wore a small polite smile on her face. He totally ruined that facade, however, when he said, "I'd like it to be."

She swallowed.

He should have backed off, but suddenly, he realized that he wanted nothing more right now than to take this woman out on a date—no matter where it was.

Turning into the gravel driveway in front of an Acadian-style house, he decided she wasn't going to answer.

However, just as he shut the engine off, she replied, "I'd like that, too."

He jerked his head around.

She was glancing out the window, not meeting his gaze as she said, "But there are things right now that prevent it.... I can't...not again."

She reached for the door.

He caught her arm. "I'm sorry, Stephanie."

She shook her head. "It's not you. I have certain things that I don't allow, and right now, dating you, it isn't allowed."

Frustrated, he wanted to ask why, but he didn't.

She opened the door then paused. Glancing at him, she said, "I wish I could explain, but... I think God sent you into my path, Ben. I really do, and I'm not sure why. But maybe later..."

Ben shook his head to stop her. "Don't say anything else. If you're ever ready for more than just friendship let me know."

It was the only thing he could say. He couldn't explain the disappointment he felt. From the time he'd carried her out of that house, he'd felt their lives were intertwined somehow. Talking, joking and laughing with her had felt so right, like she was filling a part of him that needed filling.

Pushing his door open as Stephanie helped her daughter out of the vehicle, he had to admit that even a day ago he would have said no, he didn't have any empty spots that needed filling.

But today, after the service, after all he had heard...

Was he incomplete? He'd felt empty in the service, wanting something more...but what could it be? Could it be as simple as his spirit needing to be filled with life?

Confused and a bit frustrated, he started toward the house. The door swung open.

"Stephanie! Ben! I'm so glad you're here." Sunni came hurrying out onto the porch, her kids scooting past her and down the steps to greet Katie. Dressed in a pair of blue cotton pants with a soft yellow top, Sunni had her hair pulled up and pinned away from her face. Flour dusted the front of her top, and she used a kitchen towel to dry her hands and brush off the flour.

Stephanie smiled. "Glad to see you again, Sunni." And she meant that. Her heart was distressed over the confrontation with Ben. She found she really was attracted to this man—*really* attracted. But he wasn't a Christian. And she wouldn't date someone who wasn't a Christian. Her life had been ruined because she had married a man who was a social churchgoer. The mere thought of getting involved with someone who wasn't a Christian, and who wasn't used to kids, terrified her. And she was divorced. Her husband had left her. She wasn't sure why, but she felt so much guilt.

She couldn't tell Ben all of that, but she hadn't really told him no, either. He'd left open the possibility that they might date later—but how could she?

They had to get her house ready so she could move in. Her emotions, and her daughter's, were getting too tied up in this man.

"So, how was church?" Sunni asked, glancing to her brother and then giving him a hug.

"It was...different," he finally said.

Sunni lifted a delicate eyebrow. "Oh?"

Grinning, she headed up the steps, moving aside as Veronica and Justin rushed past with Katie in tow.

Holding the door for Sunni and Stephanie he said, "It's not what you see on TV sitcoms or hear referred to in the media."

Stephanie silently groaned, worried about what might come next. She had no idea what Ben's reaction to the service had been. She'd tried to sneak a peek during the preaching, but his features hadn't revealed much.

"Dinner is almost ready. The table is set, so let's sit down in here while the vegetables finish and you can tell me what you meant by that cryptic remark."

All the windows were closed, and the ceiling fans blew cool air around in the living room.

Sunni had a nice house, braided carpets on the floor, comfortable, if old, furniture in muted tones sitting in a semicircle around a fireplace. Stephanie crossed to one of the plush chairs and seated herself.

"Take off your shoes, make yourself at home," Sunni offered.

With anyone else, Stephanie might have politely thanked her and remained on her best behavior. But with Sunni she had felt an instant camaraderie, so she did slip off her heels. "Thank you," she murmured.

Sunni dropped to the sofa and folded her feet under her. Ben sat in the chair at a right angle to his sister. Even though he was directly opposite Stephanie, the tension in the room was nearly unbearable.

Had it not been for the fact Sunni had invited them over and prepared a special meal, Stephanie would have made some excuse to leave. Instead, she decided to make the best of it and try to forget for a while her stupid words in the car.

''So, explain,'' Sunni demanded of Ben.

Ben kicked off his shoes and propped his feet on the coffee table, such an easy action she had a feeling he'd done it many times before. ''We walked in and it wasn't quiet. People stood around chatting, like at a party, conference or get-together. I have to say everyone was really friendly.''

Sunni's eyes widened. ''Wow.''

Ben grinned at his sister. ''Yeah. We sat in the third row—''

''Third row!''

Ben cut his gaze at Stephanie, still grinning, which caused her to relax considerably. He didn't look too upset. "She didn't want to be distracted by teenagers talking."

"In church?"

Ben chuckled. "Yeah. Though I never noticed anyone talking. There was some shouting, though."

Sunni's confused expression drew more laughter out of Ben. "I'm teasing you, Sunni. Boy, does it feel nice to get back at you."

She hit him with a pillow.

"No, seriously, people didn't mind at all saying 'Amen' or 'That's right' as the preacher talked. What I found interesting was the music. The songs they sang...some were fast-paced, some slow, others sounded rocky. It was interesting. I didn't know any of them, but I found it nice to see people enjoying themselves."

"In church?" Sunni repeated.

"Yeah, most of the people looked like they really liked being there. Then the preacher came up, and he was loud and liked to laugh and talked about trusting God."

A bell went off in the kitchen. Sunni shook her head. "I may have to go just to see what you're talking about. I can't imagine what you're describing.'' She got up and headed into the kitchen.

Ben's gaze drifted and settled onto Stephanie.

''Did you enjoy it?'' she asked.

Ben studied her for a moment. She couldn't read what was in his gaze. His deep, steady stare felt like it went into the depths of her, probing as she waited for an answer.

''I have a lot of questions about it.''

''I'll answer them if I can,'' she said.

''I'm not sure you can.''

She shifted uneasily. ''The Bible might have the answers.''

He shook his head. ''Give me time, Stephanie. There are a lot of things going on in my mind right now. When I get home I want time to digest everything I've heard. Then we can talk, and maybe you can help explain this Jesus thing to me.''

She nodded, hope suddenly replacing her earlier fears. Was it possible that he really meant what he said? He didn't sound like he was faking it simply to be what she wanted—like her husband had.

''I'm sorry, Ben,'' she whispered.

He stood and crossed over to her. Kneeling in front of her, he reached out and caught her hand. "Don't apologize." His deep voice seemed to rumble through him, causing her hand to vibrate in his.

She gulped at the proximity of the man she was so attracted to. Her emotions were a roller coaster since those fateful words, "It's a date." And this certainly didn't help.

"Don't be sorry." He ran a thumb over her fingers, studying her hand. "I think I'm beginning to understand what you meant, Annie mine, and if I do, then my admiration for you is growing by the minute. It takes a strong woman to stand by her conviction."

She shivered and felt tears fill her eyes. Forcefully she blinked them back.

"Stephanie," she corrected, attempting to smile.

He glanced sideways at her, cocking his head just so, and she realized at that very moment she was in trouble. She could easily love this man, this gorgeous, simple man.

"Annie," he said, and she couldn't help but chuckle.

"I'm *not* sorry," she said, knowing exactly why he'd called her Annie.

"Good enough, Stephanie," he said.

"Dinner's ready! Oh! Proposing? I didn't even know you were dating."

At Sunni's words, Ben dropped Stephanie's hand. Stephanie flushed a bright tomato red. She could feel it as it worked its way up her face. They both stood.

Ben turned, smiled a predatory smile at his sister and said simply, "You have the worst timing. So tell me, did Ronnie set the table?"

"It's Veronica!" Sunni said, and with that things were back on an even keel. The tension was gone as Sunni started berating her brother for that awful nickname.

Now if Stephanie's heart could return to neutral where it'd been before everything had happened, before she'd ended up in this man's arms being carried from a burning house, before he'd saved her daughter... She had a horrible feeling, however, things would never go back to the way they had been. Things had shifted, and there was no way she could shift them back.

Chapter Eleven

Children tell the truth at the most inopportune times.

—Ben's Laws of Life

Ben sat in his room, his feet propped on a footstool, the balcony doors open, the Bible open in his lap.

Rubbing at the bridge of his nose, he again studied the lesson he'd found in the back of the Bible, the one on the salvation scriptures and leading a Christian life.

He'd spent three hours cross-referencing everything about salvation, and the more he'd read, the more enthralled he had become.

According to the notes in the study section of this Bible he was reading, scholars who had lived in Jesus's time reported that He had lived, died and then risen again.

Logically Ben tried to think of anyone else who had had such an experience. He'd heard accounts of people who had died on operating tables and then been revived. The difference with this was Jesus had been dead for three full days, not just hours.

But if a regular person could be declared dead and come back to life, then it was certainly possible for a person that was truly the Son of God.

What he really found fascinating, however, was that the Old Testament was a foreshadowing of what was to come. The entire Bible fit together seamlessly.

If this was really true...if the Bible could really be believed, then that meant there was a heaven and a hell and that he was on his way to hell.

He couldn't stop reading. He didn't feel like stopping for dinner, or for anything, for that matter. He wanted answers, and the Bible was where he would find them.

"Whatcha doing?"

Ben glanced up to see Katie standing in front of him on the patio, Mike the Tiger gripped in her arm.

Startled, he wondered what to tell her. "I'm reading," he finally said. Glancing around he asked, "Where's your mommie?"

Her eyes slid away. "She's still sleeping."

"Ah," he said sagely. "You sneaked out of your room?"

"I have a Bible," she stated, and pointed at his book.

Glancing at his Bible, he was surprised she recognized the book in his lap. "You do?"

She nodded. Not waiting for an invitation she came in and sat on the footstool, moving his feet to make room.

He grinned.

"It tells the story about Noah and the Ark and the animals."

He nodded.

"What are you reading?"

He hesitated. He was quite shaken by what he'd read and didn't think he should tell Katie about it. "Adult stuff," he admitted.

"Like what?" she continued.

Again he paused. What should he tell her? Shrugging, he thought she wouldn't understand it anyway. "Salvation and heaven and hell," he admitted.

"Oh. That. That's not adult stuff."

"Oh, it's not?" Curiously he crossed his arms. "So tell me about it then."

She grinned and wiggled to get comfortable. Plopping Mike the Tiger in her lap, she said, "It's easy. If you love Jesus you ask Him into your heart to rule your life. You get to talk to Him every day and ask Him for help and He will teach you right and wrong. One day you'll be with Jesus in Heaven. But if you don't ask Him into your heart then you will be like those bad people in—" she squinted "—in Noah's time. I don't remember the city. But they liked to drink and have parties and didn't pray and they died in the flood and are in hell now because they didn't love God."

Stunned, he stared at the little girl. "You understand all of that?"

She nodded. "I have Jesus in my heart. I pray to Him every night."

For the first time Ben started feeling something break in his heart. This little five-year-old girl knew of Jesus, trusted Him and loved Him and didn't see anything wrong with it at all. Why hadn't he ever heard about this? Why hadn't he heard that salvation was this simple? He had thought all there was to being a Christian was being good and going to church—not a personal relationship with a living person, God incarnate.

"Do you have Jesus in your heart?" Katie asked.

Ben gulped, feeling a knot form in his throat. "I had never heard about Jesus until today," he admitted. How did he explain that the Jesus he'd heard about was a baby that grew up and died? Not what he'd heard at church or read in the Bible—not someone who was real and cared.

Katie frowned. "You don't have Jesus in your heart?"

Ben simply sat there. He couldn't answer her if his life depended on it.

He began to shake. He thought of all the information from the day, from the past weeks with Stephanie, all the facts, including the preacher's words that salvation is free to everyone.

"Why?"

He blinked at her. "Why what?" he asked, fighting to listen to her and deal with the truth that was ringing clearly in his brain.

"Why don't you have Jesus in your heart?"

Something he'd read about a child, being like a child, made so much sense now. She accepted it was the way of things, just like he had to accept it. If he did, then...something would change, that spirit part would wake up, and God would change him. He didn't understand how, but suddenly he felt the worst of sinners, having spent his entire life living as he wanted, not even realizing that someone had died for him.

Embarrassingly he felt tears fill his eyes.

"It's okay," Katie said, and came forward. Shoving at one of his hands, she climbed in his lap. "We pray a prayer every morning in Sunday school. You can pray it with me and then you won't have to be sad."

His arms automatically went around Katie to steady her.

"Close your eyes and say," she continued, "'Dear God, I have done bad things and I know it. You came and died for those things and I want You to live in my heart.'"

Ben opened his mouth to pray, but he couldn't. Not a word came out.

All he could picture was this man—God's Son—on the cross for him. Hanging there, dying, looking at him and saying, "If you were the only one, I'd do it for you."

He hugged Katie close to him. "Thank you," he whispered and then heard a low groan, more like a sob, escape his lips.

"It's okay," Katie whispered and patted him on the back.

That small hand on his back patting him was his undoing. He silently wept as the vision of him standing before his Savior, a living Savior at God's right hand interceding for him and all he had done, filled him. He shook so hard he was afraid he'd scare the little girl, but she just kept patting his back and then talking about church and Jesus and other things he didn't really hear.

Silently he said over and over and over, *I'm sorry. I'm sorry. I'm sorry. I didn't know. This is true. I've never had such a reaction to anything I've read. In my heart, deep in my heart*

*I know it's true. It's in Katie's eyes, in Steph-
anie's glow. You're real, Lord God of Earth
and Heaven. Forgive me. Show me how to be
saved. Show me how to do it.*

He wasn't sure how long he sat there until
suddenly within him a light—small but
steady—began to burn and then grow, warm-
ing him from within. As it grew the pain and
disillusionment of years faded away, and an
unearthly peace filled him.

Then Katie was pulling on his sleeve. "I
gotta go or Mommie is going to wake up and
find me gone."

He glanced down and realized he still held
Katie on his lap. Leaning down, he kissed her
on the forehead. "Thank you, sweetheart. You
go now."

She slid from his lap and left.

And then he discovered, when he was finally
alone, what real worship of God was all about.

Chapter Twelve

Just when you think you've got a handle on everything, someone takes that handle from you.

—Ben's Laws of Life

It was a very eventful time. Realizing I had feelings for my houseguest, finding out that the munchkin had gotten under my skin and I liked having her around, discovering what life was really all about. Too many things in that one day hit me and threw me for a loop.

Especially salvation.

I was rather embarrassed that I'd cried but,

hey, it was hard to explain, the feeling inside, the feeling of freedom.

Besides, it'd only been Katie and me in the room. I should be able to forget it and just deal with the rest of what was happening, or so I thought.

Little did I realize that five-year-olds don't understand tactfulness.

"Uncle Ben was bawling."

The dead silence that followed that announcement at the dinner table would have been humorous if Ben hadn't felt his face heating up at that bald declaration.

Stephanie, who had lifted a fork of her homemade spaghetti to her mouth, paused, her gaze shooting to Ben. "Ah." She lowered the fork.

The look on her face as she glanced to her daughter made his embarrassment more acute. He could tell she was trying to find a delicate way to tell Katie it was none of their business—if it had happened.

He swallowed a mouthful of food down his suddenly too-small throat. He decided to explain when dear sweet little Katie continued. "He got saved."

The words dropped like a bombshell between them.

Stephanie's eyes widened, and her mouth opened in stunned surprise. "Today?" she asked, her gaze riveted to his.

He started to answer, but Katie filled in for him. "Right in his bedroom. You was asleep but I was in there talking to him."

"Really?"

The question was directed at him.

"Yep," Katie answered.

Giving in to defeat—obviously he wasn't going to have to explain this, or get the chance with Katie in the room—he simply nodded. He wasn't sure what Stephanie's reaction would be but figured he'd just sit there and watch Katie explain it all to her mom.

He hadn't expected Stephanie to burst into tears.

But that's exactly what she did.

And noisy ones, at that.

"Uh…" He shoved his chair back and stood. Tears. He hated tears. He couldn't *stand* tears.

"Don't worry, Uncle Ben. She does this all

the time,'' Katie informed him. "Can I be excused?''

Rubbing his hands on his pants, he nodded.

Katie took advantage of her mom's face buried in her napkin to run out of the room toward her bedroom to play.

"Stephanie? Aw, come on, honey,'' he said.

He went around the table and knelt on one knee. "Don't do that.''

Reaching out, he pulled her into his arms.

She felt so right there, he realized as he patted her back. Petite, she fit him perfectly—if she'd only stop crying. Somehow, though, holding her gave him great comfort.

The warmth of her body, the wetness of her tears as they soaked his collar. "It's okay. I mean, uh...'' What could he say to the woman?

"I'm—'' sniffle "—so—'' sniffle "—happy.''

Ben blinked.

He hadn't expected her to say happy.

That warmed him.

Actually, he wasn't sure what he'd expected her to say. But as the tears slowed he eased up his hold on her so she could look at him. Her eyelashes were spiky wet with tears, the tip of her nose red. Her lips puffed out and quivered with emotion.

Kneeling there, staring so intently at her, he didn't plan it, it just happened.

Glancing up and seeing the joy in her eyes, he thought how beautiful she was, even when she cried, and without thinking he leaned forward slowly, not rushing anything, but simply acting on impulse. He moved toward her until there was no room for a tear to slip between their faces and he touched his lips to hers.

Her lips parted in surprise.

He started to pull back, but her surrender gave him all the encouragement he needed.

Ever so gently he molded and caressed her with the warmth and feeling inside him, so many emotions wanting to share themselves with her as he sealed his lips to hers in a kiss of commitment.

The intensity of her response encouraged him to deepen their kiss. It'd been too long, he realized, way too long since he'd dated a woman or felt anything for one. He'd never felt this strongly, he realized vaguely. Forcing himself to break it off, he pulled away, shaken by the intensity of feelings that rose within him.

Resting on his heels, he let out a breath.

Stephanie's eyes were wide with stunned shock as her hand went to her lips. Her mouth formed an Oh of surprise.

He nodded. "Yeah."

Clearing his throat, he stood.

She did, too, awkwardly.

"That wasn't the best timing," he offered.

She shook her head. "It certainly wasn't."

He paused and reached out to tip her head up. "But I'm not sorry."

Her eyes slid away from his, and she cleared her throat. She clasped her hands in front of her. Finally, she whispered, "Nor am I. But," she added and looked at him, "that can't happen again, not while I'm living in this house."

He agreed. Boy, did he agree. He knew on some basic level that it was important not to push this relationship too far too fast.

Stunned at the difference in his attitude, he realized something inside him had indeed changed—which made him really glad he could say the next thing to her. "We have most of the living space of your house ready for you to move into tomorrow.''

''What?'' Stephanie gaped at him.

He'd shocked her. ''I was going to tell you after dinner, actually, but, well, this hasn't been a normal day.''

He shrugged sheepishly. He sounded like a school-age boy. It was embarrassing. The entire day had been *different*. What could he say?

Stephanie's face cracked into a grin, then she giggled. Covering her mouth to stifle her mirth didn't work. It turned into a full-fledged laugh. ''It sounds as if it hasn't been a normal day in *any* sense of the word.''

Ben found himself returning the smile, relief blossoming as he realized she didn't care that he had made a fool of himself in front of her daughter. She was happy that he'd found such joy. ''Why don't we finish dinner and then we can talk about getting you moved back into your house?''

Stephanie flashed an award-winning smile at him but waved a finger. ''First, I want to talk about your day. And I expect you to tell me how my little girl ended up in your bedroom to witness your being saved.''

That look on her face as she asked, the gentle smile and warmth as she talked about Katie and asked about his day made him hear wedding bells in his head.

Mentally pulling his mind into submission, he reminded himself that marriage didn't work. Maybe in the beginning, but eventually it always turned bad. His parents' marriage had, Stephanie's marriage had. Many others he knew had.

But still, it didn't hurt to wish deep down inside that maybe, just maybe he had found someone with whom marriage would work.

But not now. Now he had to concentrate on answering Stephanie's inquisitive queries. Now he had to share what had happened to him, share the new thoughts and ideas that were suddenly swirling in his mind.

Now he had to share his heart.

Chapter Thirteen

❧

*Sometimes the only way to get an answer
is just to ask the question.*
                              —Ben's Laws of Life

Staring at the support beams where her ceiling
used to be, Stephanie asked, "Is this secure
enough to stay in the house?"

The beams had all been replaced, and the
roof was on. The wiring had been fixed. They
still had to put her ceiling in. Only half of it
was covered with plastic at the moment.

Her daughter's room was stripped of everything that could go. Anything salvageable had
been shoved under a tarp in the corner.

The door could be kept closed so the air-conditioning would work efficiently. But right now, and for at least another week or two, Katie wasn't going to have a room to sleep in at night.

"No one is going to be able to break in at night—including night critters—if that's what you mean," Ben said, and kicked at a loose nail on the floor. "I'd suggest you not let Katie play in here, however, in light of the ongoing construction."

Stephanie toed the sawdust on the bare floor. "And messy, too," she murmured. "I'll make sure she doesn't get in here." She chuckled. "Or as much as I can. You know Katie."

Ben chuckled, too. "Yeah. She can sure get away from you fast and find stuff to get into."

Silence fell between them.

Ben slipped his hands into his back pockets and glanced at the ceiling, or lack thereof, again.

Stephanie watched him.

Since he'd told her all about his experience yesterday she had been studying him. He was still the same Ben, but different. She had seen an immediate change in him, a softening, a gentleness, and a shining in his eyes that hadn't been there before.

Yet he still chatted about the same things, had the same old habit of tossing pads of paper around and walking through the house muttering, only to pause by one of those pads of paper to make a note before continuing on his way.

It was exciting to see the minute changes, however.

She'd gone to bed last night overjoyed at the new peace she'd seen in his eyes.

And yet today...

Watching him scuff the floor before walking to where the new window was, she sensed something was bothering him. He didn't have the easygoing look he normally wore. He kept stealing glances at her when he didn't think she'd notice.

She wasn't sure what that was all about.

"Would you go with me tonight to a movie?"

He stood staring out the window, so still and quiet that she wasn't sure, at first, she had heard him correctly—if at all.

"Excuse me?"

He turned, his gaze boring directly into her. "I want to take you out on a date tonight, Stephanie. You and me. To a movie."

Having been interested in him for a while, Stephanie would have sworn she would immediately say yes. Maybe that's why she was caught off guard when she said, "If Katie can't go with us, then I can't go."

Stunned at the defensiveness in her words, she wondered how her old fear about dating and marriage had managed to rear its ugly head.

She started to apologize, but Ben beat her to the punch. "I'm sorry, Stephanie. I meant...of course Katie is invited. I just thought you might enjoy a movie."

"An early show?" she asked and then really wished she had not said anything. She sounded as if she didn't want to go at all.

Forcing herself to get hold of her emotions, she reminded herself Ben was not her former husband. He was not trying to set something up and then not show. Ben was being honest and caring, not doing this out of some obligation.

As much as she liked Ben, she had to remind

herself that dating was a process of talking, getting to know one another, then going places together. It was a normal progression.

Obviously Ben had seen her interest and was acting on it. He was asking her out on a date, something she hadn't done since the break with her husband.

Now that he was a Christian, there was nothing holding her back from going with him. Except that she had fallen in love with him.

"Better early than late," he quipped.

She took a deep breath, then let it out. She hadn't been ready for that revelation about her feelings for him. It had come to her in a flash. She loved him. He must have been starting to get second thoughts about asking her out as she stood there and didn't answer. "I'm sorry, Ben. I didn't mean to sound so prickly—"

"Except you've been hurt before," he said as if he understood.

She nodded. "I would love to go out with you. And if you'd like me to ask your sister or…someone to watch Katie, I suppose I could find someone." She didn't know whom she could ask except for Sunni.

"Not at all. Katie has grown on me," he

said, and offered her one of those drop-dead gorgeous smiles that melted her heart and caused her toes to curl in her shoes.

Reaching out, he took her hand. She didn't object as he pulled her forward and guided her toward a sawhorse. "Tell me about your ex-husband."

Stephanie kept her gaze on her hands as she tried to think how to describe him. "You mean, of course, other than what I've already told you?"

"Yes."

Ben moved a box over and seated himself on it, then waited.

She shrugged. "I'm not sure what you want to know."

"What attracted you to him?"

Stephanie smiled briefly. Ben and her husband were so different. She knew that, and yet they were both businessmen. She did indeed remember her first realization that she loved her ex-husband. It had been so different than her sudden awareness of her feelings for Ben.

"What are you thinking?"

She glanced at him. "It was his ice-cream mustache."

"This I've got to hear."

At his chuckle Stephanie's smile grew bigger. "It seemed as if I'd known him forever, though that's not exactly true. We were out having ice cream with a group of friends one night after a late night of studying, and he and some of his friends were having an ice cream eating contest. And when he'd finished he looked at me and smiled and he had this white cream across his top lip.

"At that moment, I thought I couldn't do without him in my life."

Just like I now feel about you, she thought. Her smile faded. "Of course, I can do without him, but I had to learn that the hard way."

Ben reached out and caught her hand. "Through divorce."

She nodded.

"Are you over that? You mentioned to me when we first met you weren't sure."

Stephanie cocked her head in indecision. "Some days I think I am, but then Katie does something and I wish she had a father to see her accomplishment, or there's a night I have a bad dream and I wish he was there to hold me…but…"

"Him or just someone?"

Stephanie sighed and dropped her gaze. "I never believed in divorce, Ben."

Ben reached out and squeezed her hand. "It wasn't your choice. And he wasn't a Christian."

She nodded.

"I understand your hesitation in dating me, Stephanie. You're worried that I might turn out like that jerk."

She shook her head. "I—I don't think that's it. It's just...I didn't believe in divorce. It's just wrong."

Stumped, Ben stared at Stephanie. Finally he said, "You're the one that told me that God forgives?"

Her lower lip trembled. Her heart constricted. Yes, she had told Ben that. Then why couldn't she accept that forgiveness, let go of the past and embrace this man before her? She had tried to move on, but she still felt guilty. How could she really love Ben? She couldn't be what he wanted or needed. Could she?

"And I read something in the Bible about divorce last night." He was so thankful God had quickened those verses to his heart. Perhaps God did indeed play a much bigger part in a person's life than he realized as those verses came back to him. "Didn't it say something about allowing the—what did that person say, a non-believer? Allowing him or her to go? It was in…" He thought hard. "Corinthians." Sweat touched his brow as he realized he was quoting the Bible to this woman.

Stephanie stared at him, her eyes wide. "It does say that, but I'm just not sure about remarriage and…" Sighing, she finally admitted, "I feel like I've failed."

"Doesn't God forgive failure?" he asked plainly, confused by her struggle. He could understand bitterness and anger, but he wasn't sure why she felt so strongly that she had failed.

Her head dropped, her hair hiding her face. The only indication he had of her crying was a tear that dropped on the back of his hand. "Why has it taken years for this to hit home?" she whispered.

"Maybe because you haven't forgiven yourself?"

She shuddered with fresh tears.

"If God forgives, then wouldn't He forgive

your divorce and let you go on? Doesn't God give second chances?''

She released his hand and went into his arms.

Ben had said something right, he realized. Holding her close, he allowed her to rest in his arms as she struggled with and most likely was silently crying over what he'd said. Patting her back, rubbing her arm, shushing her with soft sounds, he waited, learning that this woman cried a lot. And that wasn't necessarily a bad thing.

When she was done, he could tell, because she relaxed in his arms, the tension draining from her like rainwater down a drainpipe. Slowly, carefully, she pulled back and dabbed at her eyes. ''You're right. I've allowed condemnation to eat at me for so long over this. God does give second chances, and I'm going to start today living that second chance.''

Leaning forward, he kissed her on the forehead. ''So, tell me, honey, how are you going to start living that second chance?''

Shoving her hands in her front pockets, she smiled. ''By going out to the movie with you tonight and not complaining.''

Grinning, he said, "That's the best news I've heard all day."

Returning his smile, she said softly, "Then it's definitely a date."

And this time, she really meant it.

Chapter Fourteen

❧

*A movie is the best place to find peace
and quiet—unless there are kids present.*
                              —Ben's Laws of Life

I was happy at what Stephanie had said. This
woman wasn't like any other woman I had
known. She was tender, soft, showed real emotions—even tears—when she felt them. She
wasn't the sophisticated-type woman who was
out to get a rich husband. Heck, I didn't even
know if she knew I was pretty well off. It had
never come up in conversation.

She was just a simple, everyday mother who

was doing her best to make ends meet. And somewhere along the way, I'd fallen head over heels in love with her. Okay, I know it was backward. She moved into the house, we got to know each other and then I fell for her before I asked her out on a date...but who said my life was normal?

When she'd agreed to go out with me, I'd been relieved and full of anticipation, not sure what to expect. Of course, I should have known, with Stephanie, not being that type of woman, we wouldn't be going to some sappy romance, which I had prepared myself for, and not even an action adventure.

Nope. With Stephanie, it was, of course, something we could all enjoy, which only showed me one more facet of her character.

She was a loving, responsible parent.

And boy, was I surprised when I had the time of my life at that movie.

"Uncle Ben, you want some popcorn?"

Ben grinned as Katie pulled him toward the concession line. "Sounds good to me," he said and grinned at Stephanie.

She pulled her wallet out, but he stopped her with a hand over hers. "My treat."

Stephanie shook her head, feeling her cheeks tinting pink. "I'm trying to get used to this."

Ben ordered popcorn and drinks for them while Stephanie watched Katie chatter nonstop about going to a movie. "It's been too far between movies," she said, feeling guilty for not having taken Katie more often.

"But we *are* here," Ben replied mildly.

Stephanie basked in the warmth of a date with Ben. She had enjoyed every minute of it so far, every minute, that was, except for the longing she kept feeling that continued to build within her.

She had thought such needs and desires long dead, but they were still alive in her and had knocked down her wall of restraint from the moment Ben had kissed her.

Dead emptiness and acceptance had been replaced with a hope that maybe, just possibly, once again, she might find something real, someone real.

She had told herself she wasn't going to think that way, but somehow this man had slipped under her guard, and she wasn't only attracted to him. She was in love with him. Most probably from first sight, she admitted.

Watching Ben with Katie had shown her how it might be possible to have someone in her life again. Longing and desire touched her as she remembered how wonderful, for a short time, at least, with her ex-husband, it had been to have a man around.

Ben was different however, from her ex. Ben was fun-loving and liked Katie. He didn't complain and wasn't so consumed with his job that he was never home. And she had no doubt his new relationship with Jesus Christ was real.

Watching him had sparked something within her, and after their talk at her house, she had spent a good part of the afternoon in prayer, recommitting herself to a closer walk with her Savior. She felt refreshed and renewed and was looking for a new life.

Ben handed her the popcorn, since Katie wouldn't release his hand, then hugged her to his side with his other arm as Katie dragged him along.

Stephanie was thrilled to have his arm around her pulling her along.

They gave their tickets to the young man

standing at the entrance at the back part of the complex where the screens were located, then they headed down the hall and into the darkened theater where their film would soon be showing.

She started to sit by Ben, but Katie wiggled right between them.

"Uh…" Stephanie tried to think how to explain to her daughter she had to leave her new best friend so Mommie could sit next to her date.

Ben's pained expression echoed her feeling.

However, it quickly disappeared, and with a sly grin he said, "If you sit on my lap, you'll be able to see better."

"Yeah!" Katie said and without waiting for him to possibly take back the offer or perhaps find he had no room in his lap, she scampered right up into the crowded space, spilling some of the popcorn as she did.

"Oh, dear," Stephanie said and reached to brush the kernels off his pants.

"Don't worry," he murmured and caught her hand. "This is better than the alternative."

A small thrill went through her at his words. When he squeezed her hand, she felt as warm as the butter that covered their treat. Still, before she gave in totally to the feeling of contentment she felt for this man, she had to warn him. "I'm not sure about that being better for you. Katie can be quite rambunctious."

"We'll be fine."

She nodded and settled in to wait for the movie to start. "I've gotten two different plans worked up for your ad campaign," she said conversationally as they watched the trivia fill the screen.

"You're fast."

She shook her head. "Not really. I should have already chosen a strategy and had a campaign half completed by now. Maybe tomorrow you can look at what I've done so far and give me your opinion."

"With as many pictures as you took of the site, I'd think it'd work."

Exasperated, she said, "Any ad can work, but not necessarily for what you're wanting. Some can even give the opposite message of what the advertiser is trying to send."

"Tsk, tsk," he replied mildly then slipped his arm around Stephanie. "I'll be glad to look at them tomorrow."

There he went again, changing on her, she thought. She was delighted with his light-hearted banter. Getting away from *his* home had been the perfect idea.

She felt absolutely wonderful sitting here waiting for the film about a fairy and a pig to start. She only wished she could read Ben's mind.

"What are you thinking, Stephanie?"

Stephanie glanced at Ben. "I was wishing I could read your mind," she said, smiling softly at him.

Ben returned her smile. "I was thinking that a movie theater is usually quiet. But with all of these kids..."

Stephanie laughed, her voice drifting no further than a row or two. "Just be glad it's the six p.m. showing. The afternoon show would have been much fuller."

Ben shook his head in amazement and adjusted Katie as she wiggled in his lap to get to the popcorn. "It's been so long since I've been to a movie, I'd forgotten."

"When's the last time you went to an animated one?"

Ben thought about that. She could see his

gaze turn inward. Finally, he said, "I've never been to an animated movie."

Stunned, Stephanie chuckled to hide her shock. "You're kidding?"

He shook his head. "Remember? I didn't have the ideal family. My sister and I could little afford things like this, and since my grandmother didn't go places…"

"I didn't realize… I'm sorry, Ben."

Stephanie's euphoria had faded in the moment of comprehension. Ben had had a difficult life growing up. She tended to forget that, because he was such an easygoing individual.

"Don't be sorry, Stephanie. The only thing I missed was the feeling of not belonging. And now, well…I've experienced that in a strange spiritual way so…"

His voice faded, and she realized he was happy. But someone like Ben would surely want a family of his own, wouldn't he? Or would he? Was he scared of commitment? "Why haven't you ever married?" she asked, and then realized that was probably not a good question for a first date.

He smiled, his gaze still on the screen. "I hadn't found the right woman."

Before she could respond to that cryptic remark the lights went down and the movie about how pigs got their curly tails started.

This had always been one of her favorite stories. Her daughter loved it, as well. The fairy appeared, and the animals all began to sing. Katie was fascinated and totally enjoyed the movie.

Only twice did Stephanie have to get up and take Katie to the bathroom.

Only once did a drink run down around their feet.

Stephanie thought the track record really good.

However, she should have known her luck wouldn't hold.

It happened as the lights came up.

Katie, so excited the movie was over and ready to get out of the theater, jumped up.

The cup holder next to Ben, which still held his half-full drink, went cascading.

He jumped, pulling Katie out of the way, but in so doing took the brunt of the spill in his lap.

''Ah!''

''Oh, dear!''

Katie's thumb went into her mouth.

Stephanie started grabbing for napkins, intending to help mop him up—then realized just where the drink had spilled. She thrust the napkins at him.

Wryly, he smiled. "Thanks." Then, seeing Katie with her thumb in her mouth, he frowned.

"Come here, sweetheart," he said, and crooked a finger at her.

Slowly she moved toward him.

He wiped his lap and set the napkins aside. Lifting her to his knee, he whispered, "Do you think I'm mad?"

Her little head bobbed up and down. She looked ready to cry. Stephanie clasped her hands, not sure if Ben was angry or not, certain he wouldn't do anything rash but feeling her heart go out to her downcast child.

Slowly he waggled his head from left to right. "Well, you're wrong. That drink actually helped make sure I don't fall asleep on the way home."

Katie frowned at him, having no idea what he meant. "You're all wet."

"And sticky," he admitted.

"You're going to be cold."

"Yeah," he said, and grinned. "But, tell you what. If you want to apologize, you can give me a big hug and we'll call it even."

Katie wasted no time, knowing an easy way out when she heard it. She threw her arms around his neck, launching herself at him and knocking him back into the wet seat.

Ben didn't complain but hugged the little girl tight, his eyes closing as he did.

She felt so good, this small child in his arms, so very good, he thought. This was something he could easily get used to.

Finally releasing her, he blew a raspberry on top of her head. "Let's go so the ushers can clean up this mess," he said to her.

Her joy restored, the little girl started skipping up the empty aisle.

"You'll be horribly uncomfortable all the way home," Stephanie said worriedly.

Ben grinned and slung an arm around her, drawing her close to his side. "Sweetheart, I could be covered in honey and feathers and not be uncomfortable if you were with me."

Stephanie chuckled and moved closer into his embrace.

Ben meant what he said. He'd had the time of his life as Katie had munched and slurped and laughed her way through the movie, gasping when the fairy had gotten tangled in the thorn bush. Then she had scolded the horse because he wouldn't help the poor fairy.

He'd thought when the pig had offered to aid the fairy because he was ugly and wouldn't lose anything from getting in the thorns he might lose his drink. She had squealed and jumped all over his lap in anticipation.

He should have moved the cup then and there.

But when the fairy had given the pig a curly tail as thanks for his help, Katie had clapped and settled back against him, and he hadn't given it another thought.

Of course, with Stephanie leaning into him during the movie and the fragrant smell of her hair drifting back and forth every time she moved, he had been slightly distracted. And each time she'd had to get up and brush past him to take Katie to the bathroom and then brush back, he had noticed her figure silhouetted by the light from the screen.

This woman was perfect. Physically, emotionally...spiritually. Even her faults were perfect, as far as he was concerned. He loved her. Faults and all. But what should he do about it?

Everything had been backward with them.

He escorted her out of the movie theater, past other patrons, then opened the car door and allowed Katie to climb into the back seat.

She immediately put on her seat belt and settled down with the tiger she'd brought with her but left in the car.

He opened Stephanie's door and lifted the edge of her floral long skirt, tucking it inside by her delicate ankles so it wouldn't get caught in the car door.

Then he went around, slid into the driver's side of the vehicle and fastened his seat belt. He pulled out of the parking lot and in five minutes was on the highway.

The back seat fell into an unusual quiet with Katie drifting to sleep almost immediately.

"She isn't used to this much excitement," Stephanie explained softly as they drove in the semidarkness.

"She certainly enjoyed herself."

"I don't take her enough."

The sad note in her voice caused Ben to frown. "You do what you can, Stephanie."

"I suppose."

There was a short silence and then, as they were passing out of Baton Rouge and into the country, Stephanie said, "I enjoyed myself tonight, Ben—a lot."

The easygoing feeling immediately left, and a very adult tension filled the car.

"I did too, Stephanie."

"I—"

"I—"

They both stopped and chuckled.

"You go ahead," Stephanie said.

Ben nodded, keeping his eyes on the road, one hand in hers, the other on the wheel.

"I confessed to you the other day, Stephanie, that I was interested in you. Really interested. I have to admit that I've never felt like this about another woman. I've never had time, with my mind on so many other things.

"But now...well, heck, Stephanie, to be honest, I think I've fallen in love with you."

A soft gasp filled the car.

"Don't say anything, honey, just listen. I wasn't going to mention this. We've done everything backward. Lived together, gotten to know each other, then gone out on a date. But I want you to know, while you sort out your feelings I'd like to continue to take you out on dates to prove to you I'm serious. This thing between us is something we shouldn't ignore.''

''I—I don't know what to say.'' She sounded breathless, as if she'd run a mile. He wished he knew what was in her mind.

''Tell me what you're thinking,'' he asked, tormented that he had said the wrong thing. What a vulnerable feeling to tell someone you loved her when you had no idea how she felt about you.

He didn't think she was going to answer. Then softly, barely above a whisper, she spoke. ''I think I'm in love with you, too, Ben Mayeaux. Madly, irreversibly in love.''

The driveway to her house was just ahead.

He released her hand and flipped on the blinker.

He turned into the driveway and pulled up to her front porch.

Neither spoke as he turned off the engine of the car.

His heart hammered at the words he'd just heard.

Stephanie loved him.

He got out and rounded the car and opened her door and then opened the back door. He released Katie from the seat belt and lifted her into his arms.

She was deadweight, not moving as he adjusted her and managed to get her onto his shoulder.

Stephanie loved him.

Stephanie walked ahead and unlocked the door. Ben brushed past her and crossed the living room to Stephanie's room, where Katie would sleep until the repairs on her bedroom were completed. He laid Katie in Stephanie's bed.

Stephanie was right behind him. She had a gown in her hand.

He paused, his gaze going to hers, their eyes meeting.

She said she loved him.

He wanted to pull her into his arms right now, but instead, he moved around her and went to check the rest of the house to make sure it was secure for Stephanie and Katie.

When he got to the front door, Stephanie was leaving her room. She came to where he stood.

She looked beautiful tonight, in the long flowing skirt and peasant top, her hair hanging around her face.

The light in her eyes as she smiled shyly at him caused a stirring in him. ''Where do we go from here?'' he asked, facing her on the threshold of her door.

''I don't know,'' she admitted. ''I guess we talk to Katie and a pastor for counseling. Or discuss... I don't know.''

He felt about as lost as she did at the moment. So, tossing aside logic, he acted on instinct. ''Well, for now, let me just do this.''

He pulled her forward and lowered his head to hers and placed a deep kiss of longing on her lips. His kiss searched and probed. Stephanie was clinging to him by the time the kiss ended.

And it left him too overheated for either of their good.

''Ah...well, that wasn't a great idea,'' he muttered and stepped into the night to put some distance between them.

She chuckled, a bit embarrassed at her reaction. "You forget, I was married once and it's been a long time, so I understand completely…" She trailed off with a knowing look.

That broke the tension, and he chuckled. "I just never know what to expect from you, Annie mine."

She growled at the nickname, and he stepped back to miss the swing at his arm that she took. "So innocent and yet so experienced." Shaking his head, he took another step back. "We'll discuss it tomorrow. Sleep well and dream about me."

"Arrogant," she muttered.

"Not arrogant, just wishful because I will certainly be dreaming about you."

She actually blushed. He grinned and turned and headed down the stairs. Nothing in the world could ruin the euphoria, the joy, the fulfillment of finding the perfect mate.

Thank you, God.

Chapter Fifteen

~≈

Storms come in all shapes and sizes, but the biggest storm of all is the one that sneaks up on you.

—Ben's Laws of Life

The next two weeks were wonderful. We decided to go through marriage counseling. The pastor at our church—that sounded so odd, our church—had offered to work with us. He went through seven different lessons, which included a discussion on finances. In our case, he emphasized divorce and healing to make sure we were both ready. Stephanie continued to work on the ad campaign, and I worked hard to get caught up on jobs I had let slide since rescuing Stephanie. One of the things I had to follow up on was the vandalism and theft incident.

We even decided that we wanted a fall wedding, which wasn't too far off. I hadn't told Sunni yet because she would, of course, go wild with wedding plans, and Stephanie hadn't told Katie yet, because she wanted Katie to get used to me. Katie was more than used to me. She threw a fit when she realized she and her mother weren't going to live with me anymore. I still chuckle over that one.

Anyway, things were going really great, or so I thought. I went into work that morning, planning to pick up the love of my life and her precious daughter—soon to be my precious daughter, as well—and take them to Sunni's for dinner, where they'd get to meet the infamous David, my brother-in-law.

But something happened, something I wouldn't understand for a week to come.

Stephanie hung up the phone—again. This was the third time this week she'd called and Ben hadn't been at home.

He'd been going in earlier and earlier.

She had really wanted him here for the talk this morning.

Shrugging, she admitted it was because of her nerves that she wanted him here.

Which was crazy.

She knew Katie would love what she was going to tell her.

"Whatcha doing, Mama?"

Stephanie glanced down and saw her daughter, in her pajamas, standing next to her, staring at her oddly.

Stephanie realized she stood by the phone, staring out toward the fenced area of her yard. "Ah, well, I tried to get hold of Uncle Ben, but he's already left for work."

Katie frowned. "I wanted him to come over here today."

Stephanie rubbed her daughter's messy hair. "He will. Remember, we're supposed to have dinner with Sunni tonight?"

She crossed to the cabinets and pulled down a bowl, went to the drawers by the sink, opened one and pulled out a spoon.

Katie climbed to the table. "Is he going to help me pick out a bed for my room?"

"He said he would, sweetie," Stephanie replied and grabbed a box of cereal. She placed the bowl in front of her daughter and filled it. She grabbed a container of milk from the refrigerator, poured it on the cereal and then placed two slices of bread in the toaster.

Bringing two glasses of milk, she seated herself by her daughter. "I want to talk to you about Uncle Ben," she said and felt the palms of her hands break out in a cold, clammy sweat.

Katie scooped up a spoonful of the flakes and casually shoved it into her mouth. "'Bout what," she muttered around the spoon.

"Uncle Ben is a nice grown-up man, Katie," Stephanie began. "Mama thinks he's one of the best men she's ever met. And sometimes, grown-up men and grown-up women fall in love."

"Like you love me?" Katie asked and shoveled another spoonful into her mouth, idly propping her elbow on the table so she could rest her head on the other hand.

"Elbow off the table, honey," Stephanie said.

Katie allowed her elbow to slip off the table.

Worrying her lip, Stephanie thought this talk wasn't going exactly like she'd anticipated. Taking a breath, she wondered how to explain grown-up love to a small child. She said, ''Not exactly. It's a different love, not at all like the one I have for you. You will always be my special love. But with Uncle Ben, this is a...well, a grown-up love, a love...''

She clasped her hands. She really wished Ben had been here, since she was making such a mess of things. Deciding to be honest and let her daughter ask questions, she said, ''Uncle Ben and I thought we might get married and make him your new daddy.''

Katie chewed the cereal in her mouth and stirred the spoon in the milky dish, staring into the bowl. She found and captured a marshmallow and with the fingers of her other hand picked it up and placed it in her mouth.

''Use the spoon,'' Stephanie said and got up to get the toast.

Katie licked her fingers and dropped that hand to her lap.

''I'd have a daddy?'' she asked idly.

Stephanie returned and buttered a piece of toast for her daughter. There was no use in buttering her slice, because her stomach had shut down. Nothing was going to make it past her throat at the moment.

"Yeah."

"I already have a daddy somewhere, don't I?"

Stephanie nearly cried. Of course Katie knew of her daddy, though she didn't really know him. She had never dreamed of facing this dilemma of having to explain about a father to her daughter. "A daddy, honey." She started trying to find the right words to explain her situation. This was a situation thousands of other single parents had faced with their children, but this was the first time Katie had mentioned her natural father. "A daddy is someone who will love you and take care of you. The man who was there when you were born isn't here anymore."

"I know. He went away like Keesha's dad."

Stephanie nodded. "Yes. He did."

"And he never came back."

"That's right. But Ben wants to marry your mommie and move in and start being a new daddy to you. Do you think you would like that?"

Katie picked up the bowl and drained the milk. She started to wipe her arm across her mouth but glanced at her mom.

Stopping in mid-wipe, Katie grabbed her napkin and rubbed it over her face. "I like Uncle Ben. Would he let me call him Daddy?"

Stephanie let out a breath of relief. "Yes. I'm sure he would."

"And he'd live here with us?"

Stephanie nodded. "Or we'd live with him."

"I'd get to see him a lot?"

Stephanie felt tears in her eyes. This was going much easier than she'd thought. "You'd see him all the time."

Katie shoved out of the chair and puffed out her chest. "I'd like that."

Stephanie wilted in relief and decided she was going to have to take another shower. Her daughter had put her through the wringer just now.

Kneeling, she hugged her daughter. "We'll talk more about it when you get home from school. Now go dress, okay?"

"Okay." Katie turned and scampered toward the hall. At the entrance, however, she paused and turned to her mom. "Mommie, it's okay if he doesn't come over today then, if he's going to come over tonight. Then we can all disgust about me calling him daddy."

Stephanie wanted to roll her eyes at how important her daughter tried to sound. Instead, she smiled. "That sounds great, Katie."

Katie turned and headed out of sight.

Stephanie returned to the kitchen and cleaned up after her daughter, realizing Katie had managed to get away with leaving her toast untouched and not cleaning up her spot at the breakfast table.

After she tidied up she dialed Ben's number at work.

John picked up on the second ring.

"It's me, is Ben there?"

"Yeah, just a minute," he said and there was murmuring on the other end.

"He'll be just a minute."

"Okay," Stephanie said, a bit disappointed but willing to wait.

She finished cleaning the kitchen and swept the floor while she waited, then gathered what she could of Katie's supplies.

Katie came out and was just about to head to the car when Ben finally picked up.

"Sorry, honey, I was in the other room. What's up?"

She was perturbed at being forced to wait so long, but she pushed the feeling aside. "Go on out to the car, Katie, I'll be right there."

When Katie was gone, she said, "I told Katie today and she said she wants to disgust it with you tonight."

Ben chuckled. "Well, I'll be glad to do that. So, how has your morning been?" His voice dropped, and the sound of it sent shivers down her spine.

"Fine so far. I'm looking forward to tonight."

"Tonight?"

At the confused note in his voice, she said, "Sunni?"

"Ah!" He chuckled. "I thought you were talking about our discussion with Katie. Yeah, that'll be an interesting time. Uh...honey I have to cut this short. We're really busy. I love you and I'll call you at lunch, okay?"

Disappointed but accepting, Stephanie agreed. "I'll talk to you then." The old feeling of hurt caused by her husband's inattention surfaced, but she forced it down and reminded herself this was Ben, not her ex-husband. He wasn't the same.

Ben paused and said, "We'll talk after Katie goes to sleep tonight."

She grinned. Their talks had mainly been sitting on the front porch, kissing and hand holding as they discussed their dreams for the future. "I look forward to that."

She hung up the phone.

She grabbed the keys, headed out to the car and drove Katie to school.

Returning home, she went into her office and finished the last touches on the ad campaign. It only took two hours.

Deciding to drop it off at Ben's office, she showered, dressed, gathered everything up, got back in the car and drove to his work. It was close enough to lunchtime that she didn't feel too badly about showing up unannounced.

The gravel road snapped and popped as she drove over the loosely packed pebbles. She pushed the parking brake on, gathered up her disks, papers and sketches and slipped from the car.

She shoved her hair behind her ears, smoothed her soft peach blouse and white pants. It was humid out, really humid. Clouds were gathering, and it looked like they were going to have a really bad storm today.

She knew Ben was busy, but she really wanted to drop the final paperwork off. She thought she would surprise him. Maybe she could convince him to take a break and get a quick bite to eat with her.

She headed up the walkway, tapped on the door and entered.

John sat there, manning the radios. When he saw her, he stood. "Hi, Stephanie! What brings you here?"

She held up the large flat suitcase-like satchel that carried most of the sketches. "The last of the campaign, ready to go."

"Great. Let's see." He walked around the desk and took it from her. Shoving a group of papers aside, he laid it across Ben's desk.

"So, where *is* Ben?" she asked as casually as possible as John opened the package and began perusing what was inside.

"Oh, I thought he called you this morning. A friend of his is in town, and they took some time off. I think he's actually at his house now, though he plans to be back this afternoon.''

Surprised, Stephanie glanced at John. "He said he had work to do."

"Oh, he does. I mean, yeah, he's busy..."

That sure sounded like he was covering up for Ben, Stephanie thought, thunderclouds building over her head as she remembered all the times her ex had coerced his employees or partner to lie for him.

"The guy he's with is actually the man he is busy with. What I mean," John said, and ran a hand through his hair then turned the piece of paper he was studying to a different angle so he could get a better look. "He's the man whom he has the business with. But he's also a friend. Ben had some of the stuff he needed at home so they were going to pick it up, go out to lunch and then come back here later, after..." Distracted, John let his words trail off.

Stephanie nodded, though her face was a mask of indifference. "I see. So, how do you think this will work?" she asked, motioning to what John was looking at. Ignorant of the anger and distrust roiling inside her or the insecurities rearing their ugly heads in her heart, John innocently studied the final drafts.

It was happening again.

The distance Ben had shown this week, telling her he couldn't talk because he was busy and then going out with a friend for hours at a time when he was supposedly hard at work. They weren't even married yet, and it was already starting.

What was it going to be like when they were married?

The phone rang in the office.

John picked it up. ''Yeah?''

He listened and then, with an odd look on his face, he held the receiver out to her. ''It's for you. About your daughter?''

Stephanie's heart leaped to her throat. She had only given this number to the school a few weeks ago, when the fire had forced her out of her house. And it was only for an emergency.

''Hello?''

''Mrs. Webber, this is Andrea at school. It's about Katie.''

''Yes. Yes, what's the matter?'' Stephanie didn't mean to sound impatient, but she could hear her daughter screaming in the background. Gripping the phone she said, "Is Katie okay?"

"We're trying to calm her, but she wouldn't listen. Can you come up here? She's terribly upset and won't stop crying. We have no idea what's the matter. She was in class and the teacher had the kids in small groups in a hands-on project and she said Katie suddenly let out a shrill scream and burst into tears. I'm so sorry. We're just not sure what's the matter."

All kinds of horrible thoughts went through Stephanie's head. There were snakes in the area. Had one gotten in the school? Had a spider bitten her? Had someone hurt her?

"I'll be right there."

She slammed down the phone.

"Is everything all right?" John asked.

Forcing herself not to panic, she nodded. "It's okay. I just... Can you have Ben call me at home? If I'm not there, he can leave a message where I can get hold of him."

"Sure thing," John replied. "I'm going to run these over to the printer now and the contractor. Your check will be in the mail."

Absently Stephanie nodded, not questioning

what check, simply wanting to get to her daughter. Something was wrong, and every instinct in her cried out to get to her daughter and find out what.

It took her less than five minutes to get to the school. She could hear her daughter's wails all the way down the hall.

Bursting into the room, she quickly located her daughter.

As soon as Katie saw her mom, she shot away from the several women trying to comfort her and ran to her. Throwing herself at her mother, she anchored her skinny arms around Stephanie's neck.

"Mommie! You c-can't. He c-can't be my da-ddy. Please!"

"Honey? What is it?" She tried to pry her daughter away to look at her, but Katie wouldn't release her neck. "Tyler said when Sarah's mommie married and she got a new daddy they sent her away and Tyler never saw her again. I don't want to leave you, Mommie. Please don't make me leave."

Heartbroken, her daughter sobbed.

"Honey, that's not what is going to happen at all."

"Perhaps you want to go in one of the offices," Mrs. Hebert, the assistant principal, said.

Grateful, Stephanie picked up her daughter and went into the office Mrs. Hebert guided her to.

"It will happen. It will. Tyler said so."

Hugging her tight, Stephanie stroked her daughter's hair.

"Daddy left, but this time he'll make m-me leave."

Gasping in pain at her daughter's words, Stephanie shushed her as she rocked her. "No, honey. Not at all. He won't ever make you leave. Daddy didn't leave because of you. Daddy just didn't love me. He never did. A real daddy wouldn't leave or make his daughter leave."

Katie moaned into Stephanie's chest, her wails having turned to soft sobs.

Katie didn't answer, though her sobs turned to shudders of pain, a pain Stephanie had no idea her daughter had carried all these years.

"Let me call Ben, and he can explain that he'll never make you leave, okay?"

Katie nodded into her mommie's chest but

refused to release her death grip on the only anchor she had in her life.

The counselor who had slipped in with the assistant principal handed her the phone.

She dialed the number to Ben's house, but no one was there.

So she dialed his work.

The answering machine picked up there, as well, which meant no one was in the office.

Angry and frustrated, she said curtly, "Ben. We need to talk. Now. This can't wait. Call me immediately at the school."

She hung up the phone.

"He wasn't there," she explained to the adults. Then she added, "We...well, we are thinking of getting married."

The assistant principal had a look of understanding on her face.

The counselor said softly, "It might be good to get some counseling first."

Stephanie wanted to snap that they were doing that, but instead she stood. "I'm going to take my daughter home and work this out. Everything will be fine. If Ben Mayeaux calls, please have him call me at home."

Both women nodded.

Stephanie didn't wait to check her daughter out. She simply walked out, her daughter in her arms.

It took five minutes for her to pry her daughter out of her arms.

The air outside had turned even more humid, and clouds had rolled in while they were inside.

In the distance she could hear the sound of thunder.

Driving home, she again told her daughter that having a daddy didn't mean leaving home.

The rain started as they pulled up to the house.

Stephanie grabbed Katie by the hand, and they rushed to the door. Once they were in, Stephanie crossed to the phone, hoping for a message on the answering machine.

There was no message.

She called Ben's office again, and again reached the answering machine.

Again she left a message.

When she hung up and turned, it was to meet Katie's tear-filled eyes.

Stephanie opened her arms, and Katie

rushed into them. "Don't leave me, Mommie. Don't leave me, too."

And her child once again broke down in tears.

Totally shaken by Katie's reaction to everything today, all Stephanie could do was hold her daughter. And as she did, and as she waited, the thunderclouds over her head built into full-blown storm clouds.

Minutes turned into hours and still the phone did not ring. And the entire time Stephanie held Katie, rocked her and softly sang a Christian song she had sung to her many nights when Katie had had trouble sleeping.

The storm raged outside, tearing at the trees, uprooting freshly planted flower beds and breaking off branches. It wasn't nearly as fierce as the tempest that raged inside Stephanie's heart.

That storm hammered away, crashing to the sound of the thunder and telling her that it was all happening again. She was tying herself to a man who couldn't even return a phone call, a man who put his work first.

It had all been romantic fun and games.

But when it came down to it, Katie was second to Ben's work.

When Katie had spent the last of her tears and fallen asleep in her mom's arms to the soft singing that had made Stephanie hoarse, Stephanie rose and took her daughter to bed.

As she tucked her daughter in, she also tucked away the dreams she'd had of happily ever after, dreams of her and Katie and Ben making three.

She tucked those dreams away and promised never again to put anyone before her daughter.

Chapter Sixteen

At life's worst, life can knock you down,
at love's worst, it can knock you out.
                    —Ben's Laws of Life

Ben rubbed the back of his neck just as the power came back on. Glancing at John, he muttered, "It's about time."

"We may have lost a few hours of work from the blackout, but at least you have the problem with the equipment cleared up. I don't even want to think how much extra money we would've had to shell out had you not finished that workup today."

"Today was the last day," Ben agreed and listened as the rain lashed the small trailer they were in.

"At least this twister missed our equipment," John said, trying to sound hopeful.

"Not the building, though. This puts us at least twelve weeks behind. We'll know more tomorrow when..." Ben's eyes widened. "I was supposed to be somewhere hours ago!"

John's eyes widened. "Hey...about that—"

Ben shook his head and stood up from his chair. "Later. Right now I have to go."

"But—"

"Later!" Ben snagged his keys as he rushed past John and out the door to his car.

He had completely forgotten Stephanie and Sunni.

Shoving the key into his truck, he wiped at the rain that pelted him in the face.

Quickly he climbed into his beat-up vehicle and started the engine.

While it roared to life, he pulled out his cell and turned on. Or tried to.

Dead.

He'd been carrying it too much lately, instead of leaving it at the office on the charger.

Tossing it into the seat next to him, he looked over his shoulder and shot backward.

Sunni would have dinner ready by now.

Stephanie and Katie would be waiting on him.

Stephanie and Katie waiting on him.

That sounded so nice.

He couldn't imagine coming home every night for the rest of his life to a wife and child.

It sure had been nice the last few weeks, before Stephanie had moved out of their... his...house.

They hadn't discussed which house she would want to keep after they married. He had just assumed they'd live in his house.

Turning the wheel, he shot out of the graveled drive and onto the road.

With her house repaired and a new coat of paint, they would be able to get a good price for it, unless she wanted to rent it out.

Personally he didn't want to do that, but right now, in the area, renting was a good way to bring in some extra income.

It was a good investment.

He'd talk to Stephanie about it later.

First he had to get there and explain why he was late.

And he had to disgust with Katie about being her dad.

That caused a small thrill of pleasure to work up his spine.

A daddy.

Him.

Who would have thought? And to such a precocious child.

Turning onto the road where Stephanie lived, he deftly avoided the larger puddles and downed branches the parish clean-up crews hadn't cleared away yet.

He noted the power was still on at Stephanie's house as he turned into the driveway.

The only saving point of today had been that no tornadoes had been spotted out this way.

He pulled up by her car, brought his truck to a quick halt, then jumped out before it had completely stopped moving.

He jogged to the door and rang the doorbell.

He should have stopped and gotten her flowers.

Stephanie deserved flowers.

She was such a wonderful woman, loving, kind, gentle.

He wanted to shower her with them.

When she didn't answer immediately, he knocked. ''Stephanie?''

Reaching down, he twisted the doorknob. The door opened as he pushed.

Stephanie stood there.

He reached out and pulled her into his arms.

''Sorry I'm late but…'' His voice trailed off. She was stiff.

''Stephanie?'' Stepping back, he looked into her face.

Fear clutched his heart.

She had been crying.

Something had happened. Someone had been hurt.

''Is Katie okay? Stephanie? Are you okay? What's the matter?''

''Why didn't you call?''

Call? He blinked at her curt words. Was he supposed to have called? Well, yeah, he was running late…. ''I tried.'' He offered her a smile, but the pain and anger in her gaze faded the smile right off his face.

''I've been here all day,'' she countered.

Really feeling uneasy, he shifted. The cool wet wind that whipped a dusting of rain onto the porch soaked him.

He shivered.

Stephanie acted as if she didn't see his discomfort.

"The cell phone is dead. I've had it out of the office too long."

"You could have called from the office on the other phone."

The chilly ice in her voice was worse than the cool drops of rain that had saturated his shirt. The dead look in her eyes as she stared through him chilled him even further. What was going on here? "Look, I'm sorry," he said, not sure why being late would upset her so. "I didn't think to. I was busy and..."

Stephanie laughed, but it was a laugh he'd never heard from her before. It was a laugh full of bitterness and despair.

"Honey?"

"Don't 'honey' me," she said, and a near sob escaped. He watched as the floodgates of her anger opened. "I was here all day waiting on a call from you and it never came. And as I waited I realized more and more what I was getting myself into, but worse, what I was getting Katie into, and I realized I can't—I won't do that.''

Realization of what Stephanie was raving about dawned on him. For some reason she was about to dump him. Denial rose in him. Strong denial. ''You don't mean what you're saying, Annie mine,'' he said, a bit desperately. ''Let's talk—''

''Don't call me that name. And you had your chance to talk earlier. My daughter is in there asleep, thank goodness. I wouldn't want her to hear this conversation. As for talking, I told you I didn't want you to call again. And I meant it. I'm not surprised you'd come by. *He* would always try the same thing. But it's over and done with.''

This time a sob did escape.

Ben reached for her, shocked, scared, hurting, wondering if this woman in front of him was the same woman he'd fallen in love with. She was upset, angry, bitter. Someone totally different from the woman he'd seen just yesterday. And he was hurting. Just as much as she was. Each word she spoke took a strip of hide off him.

Why was she saying these things? His hand reached to brush the hair off her face.

"No. Don't touch me." She grabbed the door as if she needed it for support.

He felt like he needed the door, too, at the moment.

"Stephanie—"

"Don't come back, Ben. I mean it. For Katie's sake. I won't love you. She can't love you."

She slammed the door in his face.

He staggered against the beam that held the overhang of the porch in place.

What had just happened here?

He looked around to make sure he was at the right house.

He was.

That was Stephanie's car. There were the leftovers from the fire near her trash at the end of the drive his men had cleaned up just two days before.

He shook his head, wanting to come out of some nightmare he was having.

It was the cold pelting of rain against his shirt that brought him back to reality.

He started to go forward and knock on the door.

Something was wrong.

He realized his hand shook as he reached for the door.

And his knees knocked.

She had said she wouldn't love him.

What did that mean?

His gut clenched into a knot, and his stomach roiled with emotions he refused to name.

All except one.

Fear.

He'd known it was too good to last.

His parents had broken up. Stephanie and her first husband hadn't been able to last.

Stephanie had realized it before they'd tied the knot.

That was it.

That's why she'd said she wouldn't love him.

Inside him, deep down inside, the part that had always wanted to belong cried out that something wrong with him had run her off.

And maybe it was. Because he couldn't think of anything else that would have caused her to tell him to get lost.

Slowly his hand dropped to his side.

She didn't want him.

Although he had given everything he had, Stephanie didn't want him.

Unconsciously he turned and headed down the stairs.

He didn't feel the pelting drops of rain or note that the storm was finally letting up.

All he felt was a cold emptiness inside as he climbed into his truck and started it. At that moment he wasn't sure he could bear the pain he was feeling.

He managed the nearly two miles to his house, but didn't make it out of the car before he broke down.

Hammering the wheel, he cried out to God. "Why? Is it me?"

And then he cried.

Angry, furious, frustrated, he cried for that little boy who had always hoped that one day he'd find a real family and for the man who had finally realized that dream.

He railed at God and asked, over and over, why?

As he calmed, a small inner voice reminded him that God had lost His own Son before getting Him back for a reason. And that Ben would always have Him as family. He would always be there for Ben. Ben just had to trust Him.

And with those realizations Ben slowly climbed out of his truck and headed inside.

He didn't bother to turn on the lights, but dropped his clothes and shoes piece by piece on the way to bed.

"I don't know what to do, God," he whispered as he climbed into bed, "but I do know I won't stop loving You. You will be there for me always."

Ben closed his eyes and slept.

Chapter Seventeen

*Family will never let you wallow—even
if it's what you want.*

—Ben's Laws of Life

"Ben Mayeaux, what are you doing?"

Ben cracked open an eye and focused on his sister, who had just stomped into his room, her arms full of his clothes.

"Good morning," he muttered.

"I found these." She tossed the articles in her arms onto his bed.

"Ow!" A shoe hit him in the chest.

"On the floor in your living room."

He rolled onto his back and rubbed his chest, opening both eyes.

"*My* living room floor," he mumbled.

"Your living room looks like a pigsty," she returned, and left the room.

He shoved up in bed and glanced around at what she had thrown at him—only to see her coming back with another load.

"Hey—"

Stuff hit him square in the face.

"Wait."

"Wait?" Sunni demanded. "Wait! I don't think so. You stood me up last week at supper. Since then I found out you and Stephanie aren't talking. She walks around like a ghost in her own house, as if part of her is dead, and your partner John says you aren't any better off. I want to know what happened. Now."

"It's none of your business," Ben said testily and shoved some of the clothes onto the floor. Finding one of his tennis shoes, he threw it to the other side of the bed. Lifting a shirt he sniffed, wrinkled his nose and tossed it at the clothes hamper near the door.

"None of my... Listen up, little brother.

When you lock yourself in your house, ignore my calls—''

''I haven't locked myself in. I go to work.''

''Physically, maybe. At any rate, I gave you a week. Now it's time to talk.''

Sunni walked over and plunked down on the end of the bed, making it jerk.

He glared. When Sunni was in this type of mood, she wasn't going to leave him alone. It meant she was gunning for him, and he was going to have to answer her. He didn't want to tell her the story of the fool he'd made of himself. He didn't want to say he'd fallen in love and gotten dumped.

''You do remember what today is, don't you?''

He didn't want— ''Huh?'' Thinking, he could only come up with, ''Friday.''

Sunni rolled her eyes. ''Just as I suspected.'' She jumped up, stomped into the other room and returned with a stack of mail.

''Hey, that's mine,'' he protested.

She tossed letters and advertisements at him until she came to one particular legal-size letter. ''Aha! No wonder.''

She tore it open, read it and nodded. "You're getting an award at noon today."

"An award?" Trying to follow his sister's line of thought had always given him headaches. Shoving the rest of the clothes to the side, he pushed the covers back and crawled out of bed. Realizing he held Mike the Tiger in his hand, he glared and tossed it on the bed.

He went into the bathroom, found aspirin and downed a few, then took a couple more, figuring it wouldn't hurt, since his sister was on one of her tears.

Besides, he hadn't slept much last night—the reason he hadn't gone to work today.

He was about to return to bed, but Sunni was blocking his way. Making a face at her, he retreated into the bathroom, slamming the door behind him.

"You can't avoid me like that. I used to help powder your—"

"Don't say it, Sunni," he warned and then flushed the toilet.

He washed his hands and face and brushed his teeth. The entire time, his sister continued to talk.

"The local TV station wants to present you

with an award for your bravery during the house fire. It's been in the paper, remember?''

He vaguely remembered something about that in a phone call a few days after the fire. He had discounted it.

''You have to be at the fire station at noon to accept the award. Channel Nine is going to be there to cover the event.''

Noon? ''Today?''

Was it already that close to the end of the month? Mentally he counted the days since he'd last seen Stephanie.

He sighed, and his shoulders sank. He had no idea what had gone wrong with her—with them. He missed Katie—and Stephanie. He slept with that stupid tiger every night. It reminded him of Katie and her sweet laugh every time that silly tiger would roar.

His heart ached at the thought of Katie.

He couldn't count how many times he'd picked up the phone to dial but had put it back down. How many times he'd gone out on his porch and stared down that way, watched for her car to pass, or gotten in his car and driven past her house.

He felt almost like a stalker, which was why when he got home at night he didn't go out.

He wasn't sure what he'd do if he saw Stephanie. Rail at her for the way she'd not given him a chance to explain? Call her selfish and coldhearted? Or fall on his knees before her and ask her why?

Thinking he might do the last, he stayed inside. He never thought he would be so weak as to want to beg a woman to explain her actions.

He had always been the type for casual friendships. This woman, however, had gotten inside his head and his heart. He felt like part of him had been cut out when she had excised herself from their relationship.

''Did you hear me?''

Ben glanced toward the door. ''What?''

He heard her sigh through the thick hardwood that separated them. ''You have to come out sooner or later.''

Grumbling under his breath, he opened the door. ''Okay, I'm out, so what are you doing there?''

He looked to where she had laid out clothes.

''Come on. Get dressed. You don't want to

be late. They're having an entire reception for you.''

The thought of being around people at the moment made his stomach turn. ''I don't want to do it, Sunni.''

''What?'' She turned, shock on her face. ''Well, that doesn't matter. You own a business. You're a community leader. You don't have a choice. If you had pneumonia and were in the hospital that's one thing, but this… This is an honor, and you can't just not show up.''

She was right, of course. Besides, what excuse could he give for not going? Except the truth. And he didn't want to tell her that.

Obviously the award was why she was here, not because of Stephanie, and he wanted to keep it that way.

''Okay. I'll go. Let me get dressed.''

She nodded. ''I'll start a load of laundry for you and then some dishes. Honestly, how anyone could live in such a mess is beyond me,'' she muttered as she gathered up some of his clothes and stomped out.

He took a quick shower and shaved.

He could live in the mess because he hadn't noticed it. He'd been too busy trying to figure out where he'd gone wrong with Stephanie to notice a few things like clothes or dishes.

Come to think of it, he was hungry. When was the last time he'd eaten?

He'd spent way too much time walking the floors and trying to think of what had gone wrong instead of concentrating on himself and his house.

Of course, to him it hadn't seemed like too much time, until Sunni had shown up and said his house was a mess. Since he was the only one who saw his house, it didn't really matter how it looked, did it?

He had to start over. That was all there was to it. He had always been an orderly person, with everything in its place, before he'd met Stephanie.

He'd never let anything get out of control. He'd always kept everything above reproach so no one could find fault with him.

So Stephanie had still found fault with him. That was good to know. He would simply chalk it up to life experience and start fresh today.

He put on the fresh clothes. He would go to the reception and accept the award and then, after that, his life with Stephanie would be over. He would find a different church where he wouldn't have to see her. He would do his best to forget Katie's sweet laugh and admit he had made a mistake.

He would spend more time with his sister.

At least, he told himself all this as he dressed. It kept his mind busy and off Stephanie for all of about five minutes.

And off the pain in his heart.

Maybe it was true that time healed all wounds.

"Are you ready?"

He glanced to the door. Sunni stood there, purse in hand, waiting. Only then did he notice she had a nice dress on and had fixed her hair. "David is already there with the kids. He dropped me off so I could ride with you."

"Ah." He nodded.

He slipped on his jacket, hunted up his wallet and loose change. Snagging his keys, he said, "Thanks, Sunni."

She glanced at him, surprised, then her face warmed into a smile so familiar to him that he relaxed some. He could always depend on his sister's love, no matter what.

"Always, Ben." She turned.

Together they walked to the car.

"I want to drive, though," Sunni demanded as they approached.

He shrugged. "I didn't know you liked to drive, sis."

"Today I do," she said, and slid behind the wheel.

He got in the passenger's side and slipped on his seat belt.

In minutes they were approaching the local fire station. Tables lined the outside of the station. Cars were parked along the main highway, including a news van. People had gathered, the entire town, it looked like. Cars passing by slowed down to see what the hoopla was about.

From the station a sign hung—Congratulations. It was a generic sign, but one that added to the festivities. Balloons of all colors were grouped together and tied on the ends of tables, to chairs, even on the fire truck's antenna.

Sunni pulled up at a gas station and convenience store across the street on the south side of the T where the two main roads met.

She slid out and dropped the keys in her

purse, to Ben's amazement. "I'll hold them for you. You don't want them making a bulge in your pocket for the camera."

He shook his head. "You come up with the craziest things, sis."

"Oh, look. There's David and the kids!" She hurried across the street, leaving him standing there.

With a sigh he crossed the street and launched into his public relations smile, shaking hands and chatting.

The news reporter and cameraman came over and started explaining where he would stand and what they would do and led him toward where a large crowd waited. "You're just in time. We just finished setting up," the young woman said and smiled.

"That's great," Ben murmured.

The crowd parted, allowing them into a semicircle. "Now stand right there," she said.

Ben stepped forward—and froze.

Standing there already were Stephanie and Katie.

He had no idea they'd be there.

Of course, it made sense.

So did Sunni's attitude, he suddenly realized.

She'd kept him off balance at the house to get him here without objection. She had driven, just in case he figured it out, and she'd kept the keys in case he tried to leave. His gaze cut around the crowd until he found her.

She was hiding behind her husband, who shrugged.

He was going to kill her later.

Forcing himself not to say a word, he walked over and stood where they placed him—right next to Stephanie.

Stephanie didn't say a word, either.

Katie had her thumb in her mouth.

The sweet scent of Stephanie drifted to him as they stood there.

The newscaster came to stand beside them and started talking.

He answered questions over and over again as she worked to get it all on tape. Stephanie answered questions, too. Her voice sounded hoarse, he thought.

He wondered why.

He couldn't glance at Katie without wanting to grab her and hold her. He knew the signs of stress in the child. Her thumb in her mouth was a dead giveaway.

Why had Stephanie done such a thing?

Then he was handed a plaque and was shaking hands.

He smiled again, then the reporter called, "Cut."

Stephanie headed into the fire station.

Ben didn't get a chance to say a word. She was gone that fast.

He turned to find his sister so he could throttle her and then leave, but they wanted pictures of him by the cake. And he had to thank all the people who had put this together.

It was ten minutes before he could break away to find his sister. The pain of seeing Stephanie, feeling her warmth as she'd stood next to him, smelling her sweet fragrance as it had wafted to him on the sluggish Louisiana breeze was more than he could bear.

His wounds were still very raw.

His sister didn't understand.

No one did.

"Uncle Ben?"

Ben froze at the sound of that voice. Glancing down, he found Katie, thumb in her mouth, standing there.

He glanced around and didn't see Stephanie. He couldn't turn his back on Katie and leave her standing there. Squatting, he forced a smile. "Hiya, Katie. What's up?"

"Why didn't you come disgust being a daddy with me?"

He reached out to pull Katie's hand from her mouth. Holding it, he replied, "Your mommie and I needed time away from each other."

"Didn't you want me?" she asked, and her lower lip trembled.

"Of course I did, and I do. You are the best little girl in the world."

Katie sniffed then blurted, just as she did the day Ben found the Lord, "Mommie bawls a lot."

Ben shook at that direct statement.

"She especially bawls at night. I hear her talking to God. She's sad. I didn't mean to make her sad."

Ben frowned. "You didn't make her sad, sweetheart. Uncle Ben did that."

Katie shook her head. "Tyler told me if I got a new daddy that you would make me go away and I'd never see my mommie again. I was scared and cried and wouldn't say it was okay for you to be my daddy. At least, not for a while. It made Mommie sad.''

Ben furrowed his brow. "Who is Tyler?''

"He's a boy from school. I don't believe him, though. You were going to come disgust with me calling you daddy so you wouldn't really make me leave Mommie.''

"I would never do that.''

Was that what this was all about? Could it be that easy?

"Mommie said you wouldn't take her phone call. She called and called and left messages but you never called back.''

"Wait a minute, Katie. When did she call?''

"The day the thunder and lightning came. She wanted you to tell me you wouldn't make me leave, but you wouldn't. So she's sad now.''

Ben blinked. "I didn't get any calls.'' Why was he telling Katie this? He should be telling Stephanie, instead. "Honey, where's your mom?''

"She's in the bathroom crying.''

His heart hurt at that. "Can you go stand with Aunt Sunni?"

Katie nodded.

They went and found his sister. "Watch her, and you just might make up for your subterfuge," he said and handed Katie's hand to Sunni.

Turning to Katie, he said, "I'm going to talk to your mommie. I'll be right back." He bent and gave her a huge hug.

Katie hugged him back. "I love you, Uncle Ben," she whispered.

"I love you, too, sweetheart," he returned and then was gone.

He had no trouble finding the bathroom. Now that he was about to face Stephanie, his mind had cleared of the pain from the past week. He loved this woman. He loved Katie. Katie loved him. He and Stephanie were going to talk, and he was going to find out just why she left him. No more Mr. Nice Guy, he thought, and set his shoulders. He took a deep breath, said a prayer and went inside.

Stephanie was standing at the sink, splashing water on her face. "Katie—" She turned, saw him and froze. "You're not Katie. What are you doing in here? This is for women!"

"Katie is with Sunni. And I'm here for you."

Stephanie blinked.

"I love you, Stephanie, and we're not leaving here until we work out our differences."

She shook her head. "It's over. We've already talked and said everything."

She started to brush past him, but he blocked her, catching her by the shoulders. "You talked. I had no choice but to listen. Now it's your turn."

"Ben—" Stephanie protested.

He immediately released her, and she stepped back.

He stepped forward. "Our business had been robbed and vandalised. That day of the storm was the last day my insurance was willing to let me file a claim for the damages. I was out with a friend—my insurance agent—finishing up the report so that we would have free time with Sunni that night."

"I don't want to hear this," Stephanie protested and took another step back.

Ben mirrored her movement by stepping forward. "Too bad." He put his hands on his waist, shoving back his coat as he stalked her. "A tornado hit—"

Stephanie gasped.

"Yes, we're all okay. But we lost power. If you left messages—"

"I did."

"They were erased by the power loss. I have no idea what you said or didn't say. I tried to call you but my cell phone was out. I love you, Stephanie."

His shoulders collapsed. "I love you, Stephanie," he said more softly. "And I would never do anything to hurt you."

Stephanie's lips trembled. "You weren't there."

"Where?" he demanded just as softly.

"Katie was screaming. She was terrified you were going to make her leave and she'd never see me again. I needed to talk to you, but you never called me, just like *him.*"

"Him? Who? Your husband?"

Turning her head to the side to avoid his gaze, she nodded.

Ben stepped forward and took Stephanie by the shoulders. "I'm not *him,* Stephanie. I will

never be him. I love you. I want you as my
wife. I want Katie as my child. Unlike him,
who deserted you, I want children—though I
didn't know it until I met Katie. I want *her* as
my child. I want *you* as my wife. I think God
brought us together for a reason, honey. That
fire not only brought me to the Lord, but it
brought love into my life—it brought *you* into
my life.''

Stephanie gasped in a breath.

''Don't you understand, Annie mine? I can't
live without you.''

At his nickname she turned and fell into his
arms and started to cry.

He hugged her close, shuddering. Oh, how
he loved her tears, he thought, and held her
tightly.

''I hope this means yes?''

Nodding against him, she mumbled into his
coat. ''Yes, yes…oh, yes.''

Relief flooded through him. The hurt he'd
experienced from that night disappeared. Lifting her face, he looked into her eyes. ''You
just keep on saying that.''

She smiled. ''Yes, yes, yes, yes—''

He cut it off with his lips over hers, sealing
the bargain for now and evermore.

Chapter Eighteen

Life is just great when you're with the one you love.

—Ben's Laws of Life

"Daddy, the ring."

Ben glanced down at his soon-to-be daughter and smiled. Taking the ring from her, he smiled at Stephanie.

"The ring, please," the pastor said.

She was so beautiful. The ivory dress she wore touched the floor. It had a high waist and floral embroidery on the bodice and the sleeves. Her hair was pinned up and adorned with flowers. But the most beautiful sight was the love in her eyes. He'd never tire of seeing Stephanie's love for him.

Placing the ring on her finger, he repeated his vows.

"And your ring?"

Justin handed Stephanie her ring. She placed it on his finger with trembling hands.

And then Stephanie repeated the same vows.

"You may now kiss the bride."

Leaning forward, he touched his lips to hers.

"I now pronounce you man and wife."

"And a daddy!" Katie yelled into the quiet.

Ben laughed. "And a daddy!" Lifting her into his arms, he turned so the guests could see him, his daughter and his new family, pride nearly bursting the buttons on his tux.

So that's how I got to where I am now, you see, and that's how I got a wife and a family.

With all the love he felt, Ben glanced back at his wife and thought, Forever more.

Ben's new laws.

When you think life is going along just fine, watch out because you'll find out that God has something special in store for you. And it just might take you through the valley and back before you find it.

* * * * *

Dear Reader,

Not too far from here there is a town called Pride, Louisiana. I thought it would make a wonderful setting for a story. Pride represents any small town, perhaps even the one that you live in. Its residents are everyday folk, people that you know.

In Pride and other communities all over the world, people become heroes by their simple actions. Giving a cup of water to someone who is thirsty or calling someone who is in the hospital or visiting someone who lives by himself or herself can be in itself a heroic act. You don't have to save someone from a burning building or from something horrific to be a hero. Sometimes the simplest act of kindness is heroic to the person who receives it.

I'm sure we all can come up with someone who is an everyday hero to us. Take time to let those people in your life know how much you appreciate them. Let them know how much they mean to you. And remember that by helping someone, you might just become an everyday hero, too!

Blessings,

Cheryl

Steeple Hill Books is proud to present
a beautiful and contemporary new look
for Love Inspired!

As always, Love Inspired delivers
endearing romances full of hope, faith and love.

Beginning January 2003
look for these titles
and three more each month
at your favorite retail outlet.

Steeple
Hill®

Visit us at www.steeplehill.com

LINEW03

Take 2 inspirational love stories **FREE!**

PLUS get a **FREE** surprise gift!

Mail to Steeple Hill Reader Service™

In U.S.
3010 Walden Ave.
P.O. Box 1867
Buffalo, NY 14240-1867

In Canada
P.O. Box 609
Fort Erie, Ontario
L2A 5X3

YES! Please send me 2 free Love Inspired® novels and my free surprise gift. After receiving them, if I don't wish to receive anymore, I can return the shipping statement marked cancel. If I don't cancel, I will receive 3 brand-new novels every month, before they're available in stores! Bill me at the low price of $3.99 each in the U.S. and $4.49 each in Canada, plus 25¢ shipping and handling and applicable sales tax, if any*. That's the complete price and a saving of over 10% off the cover prices—quite a bargain! I understand that accepting the books and gift places me under no obligation ever to buy any books. I can always return a shipment and cancel at any time. Even if I never buy another book from Steeple Hill, the 2 free books and the surprise gift are mine to keep forever.

103 IDN DNU6
303 IDN DNU7

Name	(PLEASE PRINT)	
Address	Apt. No.	
City	State/Prov.	Zip/Postal Code

* Terms and prices are subject to change without notice. Sales tax applicable in New York. Canadian residents will be charged applicable provincial taxes and GST. All orders subject to approval. Offer limited to one per household and not valid to current Love Inspired® subscribers.

INTLI_02

©1998 Steeple Hill

Next Month From Steeple Hill"s

Love Inspired

Love at Last
by
Irene Brand

On a business trip, media consultant Lorene Harvey
accidentally meets her college sweetheart, Perry Saunders.
Even after twenty years, they still have feelings for each
other. But Lorene has a secret two decades old that she
fears Perry will never forgive. Will she be able to put her
trust in faith and find the strength needed to find
Perry's love and forgiveness?

Don't miss
LOVE AT LAST

On sale November 2002

Love Inspired